MW01672287

Derek asked.

"Me?" Melissa's eyes widened. "I'm not trying to prove anything."

"Sure." Slowly he trailed a fingertip down the side of her throat. "If you wanted me to realize how you've changed, you've succeeded."

"I . . . I don't know what you mean," she stammered.

"I think you do." He smiled knowingly. "What I'm wondering is how far you're willing to go to keep me from taking you home."

"How far I'll—" Her eyes widened as she realized what he was saying. Darn the man! Why couldn't he understand all she wanted was for him to see she was no longer a child? "If you mean will I sleep with you, the answer is you're crazy, Vincetti."

"Am I?" He dropped his hands to her waist and pulled her to him. . . .

Dear Reader,

It's May... it's springtime! Flowers are in bloom, love is in the air... *and* on every page of this month's Silhouette Romance selection.

Silhouette Romance novels always reflect the magic of love in compelling stories that will make you laugh and cry and move you time and time again. This month is no exception. Our heroines find happiness with the heroes of their dreams—from the boy next door to the handsome, mysterious stranger. We guarantee their heartwarming stories of love will delight you.

May continues our WRITTEN IN THE STARS series. Each month in 1992, we're proud to present a book that focuses on the hero and his astrological sign. This month we're featuring the stubborn, protective Taurus man in the delightful *Rookie Dad* by Pepper Adams.

In the months to come watch for Silhouette Romance books by your all-time favorites such as Diana Palmer, Suzanne Carey, Annette Broadrick, Brittany Young and many, many more. The Silhouette Romance authors and editors love to hear from readers, and we'd love to hear from *you*.

Happy Springtime... and happy reading!

Valerie Susan Hayward
Senior Editor

MARIS SOULE

Missy's Proposition

Silhouette Romance

Published by Silhouette Books New York

America's Publisher of Contemporary Romance

SILHOUETTE BOOKS
300 E. 42nd St., New York, N.Y. 10017

MISSY'S PROPOSITION

ISBN: 0-373-08864-7

First Silhouette Books printing May 1992

Printed in the U.S.A.

MARIS SOULE

was born in California but now lives in Michigan with her husband and family. The author of numerous category romances, she is now eager to try her hand at the Silhouette Romance line. Maris believes that marriage takes a lot of commitment and energy, but it is the best thing that can happen to a person. When Maris and her husband married, they decided to take one year at a time, renewing their "unwritten" contract each May. So far, they've renewed it twenty-three times—not bad in this day and age!

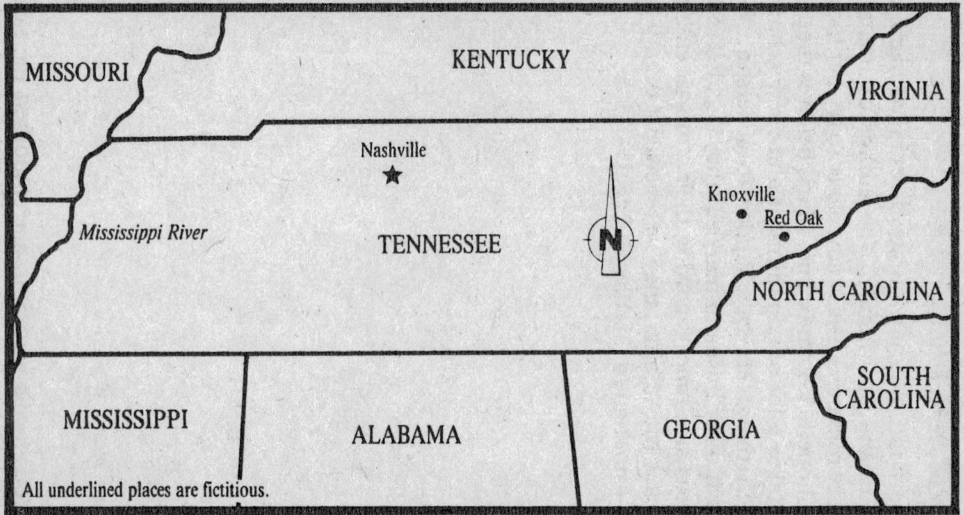
MISSOURI
KENTUCKY
VIRGINIA
Nashville
Mississippi River
TENNESSEE
N
Knoxville
Red Oak
NORTH CAROLINA
SOUTH CAROLINA
MISSISSIPPI
ALABAMA
GEORGIA
All underlined places are fictitious.

Prologue

Stanley Davenport had played golf that morning—after the women finished teeing off—had had a late lunch at the country club, then stopped by the house to change clothes before checking in at the office. The mail was on a silver salver in the foyer. It was the letter addressed in his daughter's familiar scrawl that caught his eye. Ever since the telephone call he'd made the week before, he'd been expecting to hear from Missy.

Stanley Davenport didn't go to the office that afternoon.

He was in the library, pacing a hole in the Aubusson rug, when his wife returned from playing bridge. As the maid took Helen Davenport's coat, Stanley called her into the library. He didn't give her a chance to sit down before he thrust the opened letter into her hand. "Here. Read this. It's from your daughter."

To his frustration, his wife took the time to sit in one of the matching Queen Anne chairs. As though oblivious to his agitation, she smoothed the skirt of her silk suit, took her reading glasses from her purse and put them on. Finally she looked at the carefully typed three pages.

Stanley could almost recite the contents by heart now, mainly because he simply couldn't believe Missy was at it again.

Up until last week, they'd thought she was at Cape Cod with a sick friend. A *very* close, *very* sick friend, from what Missy had been telling them for the past three months. She'd called them every Saturday with a progress report, always saying Julie needed her, and she was going to stay a little longer. It was only by chance that he'd placed that call to her last Thursday and ended up talking to Julie's mother. Surprise was an understatement for his reaction when he discovered Julie was in excellent health, had been all summer and that Missy hadn't been in Massachusetts since early spring. Since early July, his daughter had been lying about her whereabouts.

Now he knew why.

"She's in Tennessee? Working with problem children?" Confused, his wife looked up. "I don't understand."

"Obviously another of our daughter's harebrained do-gooder ideas." He'd swear every bleeding-heart cause in the world saw Melissa Elizabeth Davenport as an easy mark.

He'd thought she'd outgrown her penchant for philanthropy, that four years at Vassar had taught her people made money by hard work and sound investments, not by giving it away. He'd wanted her to study finance and business management, matters she'd have to face when she inherited his money. But no, she'd gone and majored in English and education. Still, there was no need for her to go out and work as a teacher. And certainly not in Tennessee, at a school for misfits.

Finished reading, Helen Davenport put down the letter. "What about Paul?"

"I called and talked to him less than an hour ago. He said he hasn't heard a word from her all summer. Not since she left in July." And that disturbed Stanley. "I should have checked with him before. I know Missy said she turned him down, but I was sure he'd keep in contact with her, keep trying. There's certainly not going to be a wedding with her in Tennessee."

"I feel uneasy about this, Stan."

So did he. And angry. Damned angry.

Once again Helen looked at the letter. "She says the area's very poor. Do you..." She hesitated, took a deep breath, then quickly went on. "Do you think there's a chance someone might try to kidnap her?"

Stanley knew what his wife was thinking, remembering. Missy had been six years old when she was kidnapped. For forty-eight hours they'd lived in terror that they'd never again see their baby, their one and only child. The money they'd paid that man meant nothing compared to Missy's safety.

Clenching his fists, Stanley made up his mind. "I'm going to bring her home."

For a moment the tension left his wife's face, then returned. "How? She's twenty-three years old. An adult."

"She's certainly not acting like an adult." Nevertheless, the "how" might be a problem. Missy was legally of age to live where and as she pleased. And she'd been very careful not to mention exactly where she was in Tennessee.

But they had a postmark.

And they had Derek.

"I'm going to send Vincetti. He'll find her and bring her back where she's safe."

Chapter One

Tension. It tied Melissa Davenport's stomach in knots and tightened the muscles at the back of her neck. Standing on the sidewalk in front of the Learning House, she tried to relax.

The school day was over and the students were leaving Red Oak Elementary School, but for four girls and six boys there would be more instructions, more learning. Clustering together, they headed down the sidewalk toward the two-story white house with its sagging green shutters. Unruly and unpredictable, the ten could certainly cause tension. But today they weren't the problem.

Nor could Melissa blame the weather, though it was hotter than normal for the end of September and as muggy as a steam bath. With a storm front heading their way, the atmosphere was definitely turbulent. Early fallen leaves swirled about her feet, clung to her cotton slacks and blew across the yard.

The wind whipped her long, golden-brown hair into her eyes, and she turned her head, looking away from the school. In the distance rose the Great Smoky

Mountains, low gray clouds concealing the peaks and adding to the blue, smokelike haze that almost always hung over the range. She'd heard in the spring the wild rhododendrons and azaleas that grew on the balds and along the riverbanks dazzled the eye, but this afternoon the tree-covered slopes looked washed out.

Up until July, she'd never been to Tennessee. She'd hoped to stay in Red Oak until the end of the school year, hoped to find out for sure if this was truly the vocation she wanted to follow. Eight days ago her plans had changed.

Her father had called Julie's house and talked to Julie's mother, and with that one unexpected call, Melissa's fabricated excuse for staying away from California and her parents had gone down the tubes. Thank goodness Julie had warned her.

"How long before you get here, Derek?" she whispered into the wind, her tension continuing to grow.

Derek Vincetti had been hired on to Davenport Computers' security staff the summer she'd turned fifteen. He'd been twenty-five then, single and the most impressive man she'd ever met. For her, it was love at first sight. Puppy love she'd call it now, though back then she would have sworn to one and all that it was true love.

Only she didn't actually swear it to anyone because she hadn't dared let her father know she was in love with the dark-haired half-Italian he'd just hired. The ten-year difference in their ages was bad enough, but Melissa also knew her father would never condone a union between his daughter and a man whose security check showed he'd barely graduated from high school, whose parents had died alcoholics and whose older brother couldn't keep a job. Giving a man like Derek a chance as an employee didn't mean accepting him into the family. If Stanley Davenport had even suspected his little Missy's heart skipped beats whenever she saw Derek, the man would have been out the door faster than technology changed in the field of computers.

Melissa knew her father still wouldn't condone a union between them—Paul Thorton was the man, in her father's opinion, she should marry—but the confidence Stanley Davenport had in Derek's potential had certainly proved correct. In eight years Derek Vincetti had risen from flunky to the head of Davenport Computers' security department. Tough and savvy, he could ease an unwanted visitor out of the building without causing a ruckus, could develop a security system that was tailor-made and flawless, could act as bodyguard at a high-level social function without looking out of place and could get a determined, civic-minded daughter to give up her latest crusade and come home.

And he'd be coming here to Red Oak, Tennessee. Soon. She was sure of it.

Her tension increased as the children came down the sidewalk, all ten clustered together like a small gang. Trouble came in all ages and sizes. Melissa knew what most of these boys and girls needed was guidance, discipline and love. Lots of love. She wondered how long she'd be around to supply it.

Susie Fox, the youngest, was a kindergartner. She had long, reddish-blond pigtails and an adorable smile, but if she couldn't get her way, she'd bite people. Melissa hoped to break that habit fast.

The child stopped to pick up a fallen leaf, only to have Tommy Cooper, who was three years older, snatch it from her. Susie yelled and went after Tommy, her teeth bared. Her older brother, Clint, ignored her. He and three other boys in the group were absorbed in conversation.

Melissa could hear what they were saying. She had a feeling she was meant to hear.

"It's bad enough I gotta come here. I ain't doin' no cookin'," Clint grumbled, his strawberry-blond hair limply hanging below the collar of his torn and faded rock-group T-shirt. "Pizza or no pizza."

Jim Allerton, a stocky, dark-haired boy who was already thirteen but still in the sixth grade, glared at Melissa as they neared the house. "My pa don't see no need for me to haveta go to more school than I already does. He quit and got a job when he were my age. If they wouldn't put me in juvie, I'd quit."

Melissa could imagine Jim's father telling his son to drop out of school. The man was the least supportive of any of the parents. Hank Allerton had also rarely held a job for more than six months and was currently unemployed. There had to be a way to make Jim see he needed a better education.

That was the goal of the Learning House, and Red Oak was a test area. The State of Tennessee hoped early intervention would break the cycle of ignorance and poverty. But the project was small. Gwenn Bradley was the supervisor and coordinator, Melissa the sole member of the staff.

She gave one last glance down the street. The parents picking up their children after school had come and gone, and except for a brown van parked two houses down, the street looked deserted. There was no sense worrying about the inevitable; Derek would come when Derek came. She had work to do.

"Hi, guys. Ready for a gastronomic adventure?" Melissa asked with a smile that showed the dimples in her cheeks.

"A gastro what?" Clint returned, then nudged Jim. "Miz Davenport wants gas. Whaddya say?"

Jim smiled knowingly as he walked by, and suddenly the two boys behind him started gasping and gagging. Melissa knew then they had an interesting afternoon ahead of them.

She grabbed Susie as the child ran past. The girl was still baring her teeth at Tommy. Gwenn Bradley—a tall, slender brunette in her early forties—opened the door, and the children entered the house, but Melissa felt the tingle of anticipation skitter down her spine and paused to glance down the street. Treetops swayed in the wind and the leaves on the sidewalk swirled and danced, but to the eye everything looked normal. Yet she knew there was nothing normal about this Thursday afternoon. "Where are you now?" she whispered aloud, then gasped in pain.

With Susie's teeth sinking into her skin, Melissa momentarily forgot Derek Vincetti's impending arrival.

It took a while, but by three-thirty Gwenn and Melissa had the children under control. Or at least moderately controlled. Like the storm building outside, there was no telling when these children would erupt. They'd been assigned to Gwenn's special after-school session for a number of reasons, ranging from emotional impairments to learning disorders. Put them together, and you had the potential for disaster every afternoon, five days a week.

But Melissa loved working with these children. Small steps were great victories. Little things became important, like a day when Susie didn't bite anyone; when Tommy read his first sentence; and when Clint discovered he could actually get a grade higher than a D- on a test. She was glad Gwenn Bradley's ad for an assistant had been listed in the teachers' bulletin, glad Gwenn had wanted her to help start this program.

In the three months Melissa had known Gwenn, the woman had become both mentor and friend. She could learn so much from her, and Gwenn needed someone who could work at minimum wages, share room and board and stay until June.

Only now things might change.

And all because she hadn't given enough thought to how to keep her parents—specifically her father—off her back.

Tension continued to knot the muscles in her neck and shoulders. In theory no one, neither her father nor

Derek, could make her quit this job and return to California if she didn't want to go. But her father's persistence was legendary in the computer industry, and she knew Derek. She'd heard her father's tales of how the man worked. If there was a way to hijack her without causing a ruckus or legal battle, he'd find it. It was going to be up to her to convince Derek she should stay.

Absently Melissa rubbed her nape, then glanced at her watch. Next to her watchband remained the faint bruise marks of Susie's teeth. The child hadn't broken the skin and had sounded truly sorry when she'd apologized. Maybe they were making progress. Melissa hoped so.

"Time to head for the kitchen," she said, her words directed to the four older boys.

Their response came almost in unison. "We ain't hungry."

"Maybe you're not, but they probably are." She nodded toward the younger children.

"Cookin's wimmen's work," grumbled Jim.

"Not really. Lots of men cook. Come on, boys, this will be fun. I know you all like pizza. You told me so. And I bought everything you said you wanted for toppings."

"Everything?" asked Reed Volkart, a pudgy, redheaded boy who didn't resemble a reed in any way. His rounded face brightened. He'd listed foods Melissa was sure he never got at home.

Clint looked at Jim, then shrugged and headed for the kitchen. "What the heck."

She never did get the boys to put on aprons, but once past the hand-washing stage, they forgot cooking was below them and began having fun. Punching and slapping the dough for the crust allowed Jim and Clint to take out some of their aggression, and Reed thoroughly enjoyed sampling the toppings Jerry Cole, the most hyperactive in the group, passed around before he should.

But by the time the pizzas were in the oven baking, the kitchen looked as though it had been hit by a tornado. "Okay, now we clean up," Melissa said, stopping the boys before they escaped back into the living room.

"If we gotta cook, they oughta clean up," complained Jim, pointing toward the living room and the younger children.

"Nope. You make the mess, you clean it up. I'll be back in a minute." She needed to get paper plates and napkins from the back room.

Melissa was out of the kitchen no more than two minutes. No time at all. From the back room, she could hear the boys arguing about who should do what. They always argued over everything. She also heard the doorbell ring. That was another common occurrence, even though Gwenn tried to keep interruptions to a minimum.

Then, suddenly, a debated division of labor erupted into a full-scale war. Words of anger turned into actions.

Melissa heard Jim swear, a thud, a yelp and more swearing. By the time she dashed back into the kitchen, the flour sack lay on the floor by the refrigerator, flour covered the linoleum, and Clint was throwing plastic measuring cups and emptied tin cans at Reed. At the refrigerator, Jim was at Jerry's throat.

"Stop it! Stop it now!" Melissa yelled, rushing across the room. "Stop it, all of you!"

Clint and Reed did, but Jim ignored her.

"Take it back," he repeated, banging Jerry's head against the refrigerator door.

Not even thinking, Melissa grabbed Jim by the back of his shirt and pulled. But at thirteen Jim was already taller and bigger than she was, and her effort was as effective as a fly tackling a raging bull.

"I'm gonna smash your face in," Jim growled at the younger, smaller boy in his grasp.

"Stop it!" she again demanded.

To no avail.

Jim's right hand came back, and Melissa grabbed for his arm. Her fingers gripped the boy's wrist, but she couldn't hold back the momentum of his swing. As she was propelled forward, her shoulder and the side of her head hit the refrigerator.

The first thought that crossed her mind was the enamel felt cool, very cool. Then she realized her face was moving down that smooth, cool surface. Her knees refused to hold her up, and with her shoulder still against the refrigerator door, she slowly sank to the flour-coated linoleum.

Stunned and dazed, she half-lay half-sat on the torn bag of flour. The pin-striped gray slacks and black leather shoes that suddenly filled her view didn't register. Nor did Jim's panicked yelp. All she knew was that Jim's feet were suddenly dangling and kicking in the air, and that didn't make sense.

It was the stern, unequivocal, "Kick at me one more time and you're dead meat, kid," that brought her gaze higher.

While working with the boys to make the pizzas, she'd actually forgotten the reason she'd been tense all day. Warring boys had eliminated thoughts of the other battle she'd been dreading. But staring up at the dark, glowering man holding Jim in the air, she knew her time had run out.

Like a smoldering volcano, Derek was about to erupt. His dark brown eyes were narrowed, his nostrils were flared and his mouth was a tight, straight line. Under the smooth wool gabardine of his suit jacket, the breadth of his shoulders and the ripple of his muscles stated loud and clear that he wasn't a man to be argued with. His voice was deep, whiskey smooth and lethal. "Give me one good reason not to turn you into dog food, kid."

His back to Derek, Jim Allerton opened and closed his mouth twice, but no sound came out.

"Let him go, Derek," Melissa said, her senses jarred but her body intact. Helplessly lying on her side was not the impression she wanted to make on this man, and she quickly got to her feet. Her goal was to show him she was a mature, capable woman. This wasn't a good start.

Derek obeyed her command. Opening his hand, he released his grip on Jim's T-shirt, and the boy dropped to the floor. As his feet hit, Jim's knees buckled some, but he spun around, fists cocked, ready for a fight.

And then he took a good look at the man he was facing.

Melissa almost smiled. She could see the boy measuring Derek's height and coming up with over six feet, would bet Jim was comparing Derek's build to a tackle's, and knew Jim could sense that Derek was as ready for a fight as he was. She wasn't surprised when Jim made the decision that survival took precedence over saving face. Unclenching his fists, the boy backed up until he was shoulder to shoulder with Jerry.

Who for once in his life wasn't moving a muscle. Wide-eyed, Jerry simply stared at Derek.

"I believe you boys have some cleaning up to do," said Melissa. None of the silly giddiness she felt inside was reflected in the firm tone of her voice. She knew she had to regain control of the situation. If she expected to win any arguments with Derek, she couldn't appear weak or indecisive. She just wished seeing him—that standing only inches from him—wasn't turning her already wobbly legs to rubber. She leaned against the counter for support. "I want it done now, boys!"

"Right!" said Clint from where he stood, and he immediately went over to pick up an empty can of tomato sauce. And Reed grabbed a rag and started wiping up some of the spots where the sauce had spattered the floor. It took Jerry a second longer before he found the nerve to slide to the side, away from the refrigerator and Derek. But as soon as he moved, so did Jim, the older boy's eyes never leaving Derek's face.

"You okay, Melissa?" Gwenn asked from the doorway. "I heard them arguing and was going to come check on the situation when the doorbell rang." She nodded at Derek. "He moved faster than I did. This the guy you've been expecting?"

"Yes." Melissa turned to Derek. "Once again, you've come to my rescue, Mr. Vincetti."

He looked around the room—at Gwenn, at the boys, then back at Melissa. "Looks like your father's concern for your safety was well founded."

"Normally we don't have fights around here," Gwenn said quickly, in defense of the program. "I think it's the weather. This wind seems to have everyone edgy."

"Yeah, that's it, it's the weather," Jim agreed, ready for any excuse that might keep him from getting punished. "My pa calls this a spittin'-mean wind."

Derek leveled the boy with a piercing look.

"But I ain't gonna let no wind bother me no more," Jim quickly added, moving farther away. "I ain't never gonna touch Miz Davenport again."

"You're right about that," Derek agreed. "Get your things, Missy. You're leaving."

"No, I'm not," she said firmly. The time had come to make a stand. Boldly she looked him square in the eyes. "I have a contract to work here until next June."

"Contracts can be broken."

"Only if both parties agree...and I don't agree. This is my job. I applied for it, I believe in what I'm doing and I'm not leaving. So don't try throwing me over your shoulder and carrying me out of here the way you did when I was seventeen. I'm twenty-three now. A grown woman capable of making my own decision...with or without my father's and your permission."

Derek almost smiled at her determination, and for the first time since he'd arrived, he truly looked at her.

The last time he'd seen Missy Davenport was at the company's annual Christmas party, almost ten months ago. He hadn't paid much attention to her then. That night he'd been too involved in keeping track of a wife who seemed intent on embarrassing him and everyone else at the party. That night he hadn't noticed how grown up and pretty the boss's daughter had become. And the other day, when her father had asked him to bring Missy home, Derek had only remembered how she'd looked as a teenager—all pimply faced, awkward, and overweight.

It wasn't a teenager standing in front of him now, and Melissa Davenport's smooth, peaches-and-cream skin didn't show any signs of pimples. She'd lost weight—a lot of weight—grown in height and had changed from awkward to graceful. She'd also let her hair grow. No more spikes of green; her punk phase was long behind her. Now her hair was its natural golden brown, and though a little tangled from her fracas with the boys and permed into tight curls, it fell to her shoulder blades.

There were a few things about her that hadn't changed. She still had the same aristocratic, straight nose, the same little pout to her lips and the same entrancing eyes. The color of her eyes had always fascinated him. Never truly green or brown, they were an ever-changing combination. He remembered asking her—the day she turned sixteen—what color she was going to put on her driver's license.

"I don't know," she'd said, then blushed and grinned, showing her dimples. "Maybe breen. Wouldn't that be a combination of brown and green?"

He imagined if she'd smile now those dimples would still be there. They were one of her most endearing features, along with her sweet, musical voice. Even when she yelled, her words always had a lyrical quality.

It had been four years since she'd last yelled at him. That was the day he'd called her father at home, and Missy had answered the phone. In conversation, he'd told her he was marrying Carolyn Bronson, and Missy had called him an idiot. Looking back, he had to agree with her.

Since then he'd been away the times she'd come by the plant. Or she was the one who was away—traveling to Europe, going to Vassar. Slowly he let his gaze slide down her body. What a difference a few years could make. Missy Davenport had grown into a lovely young woman. A very sexy, very desirable, lovely young woman.

That realization came as a shock, and his eyes snapped back up to her face.

Melissa smiled. She'd purposely remained silent to give him time to look at her. She wanted him to see she'd changed. That was also why she'd dressed so carefully that morning, choosing a hot pink blouse that was demure enough to be proper yet designed to accentuate her breasts and small waist. She looked good in pink, so she'd matched the blouse with pale pink slacks that showed off the results hours and hours of aerobics had achieved.

I hope you took a good look, Vincetti.

She wanted him to realize he wasn't dealing with the same girl he'd hauled back to her father six years ago. She wanted him to see her as a woman.

The smell of almost-cooked pizzas forced her to move. With more assurance than she felt, she began giving orders. "Gwenn, get the kids ready, I'll have the boys bring the pizzas in as soon as they're cut."

The boys had stopped working, but a wave of her hand got them started again. To Derek, she nodded. "We'll talk later, after the children have gone. Meanwhile, would you mind holding down the fort while I finish getting the plates and napkins?"

Derek watched her go into the other room, then he looked back at the boys. They didn't seem as unruly as they had five minutes before. The kid with the long red-blond hair was tossing empty containers into the wastebasket, the fat redhead and the scrawny kid who'd been pinned to the refrigerator were wiping off the table and counter, and the boy called Jim was sweeping the flour. They all pretended not to look at him, but he knew each boy was watching, waiting to see what he would do or say next. He said nothing.

The aroma of a yeast crust, tomato sauce, garlic and cheese reminded him of the hundreds of pizzas he'd eaten as a boy. Overcooked, dried-out pizzas that his drunken father would put in the oven and forget. He hated pizza. And he hated being used as a courier to bring back a wayward daughter. Someday soon Stanley Davenport was going to have to find someone else to run after his child. That, or do it himself.

A portable air conditioner in the living room had the temperature a little cooler there, but the oven was turning the kitchen into a hot box. Derek knew if a Ralph Lauren suit was going to impress anyone here, it had already done its job, and it was ridiculous to pretend he was comfortable wearing a jacket and tie. He pulled off his tie and stuffed it into a pocket, then easily shrugged out of his jacket and draped it over the back of a chair. Next he unbuttoned the top two buttons of his shirt and rolled up his sleeves, exposing the dark hairs on his chest and arms.

Gwenn had gone back into the living room to get the younger children ready for their afternoon snack. He knew from the people he'd contacted and the report he'd read that her name was Gwendalynn Bradley, that she was forty-four years old, divorced and had two children: a married daughter—twenty-one—who lived in Gatlinburg, and a nineteen-year-old son, who'd lived with his father since the divorce five years ago and was now away at college. The woman had taught school for fifteen years, went back for a degree in special education and administration and had been hired in May specifically for this program. From what he'd gathered, she was well respected as an educator and a person. Unlike some of the endeavors Missy had gotten involved with in the past, this one seemed to be a legitimate project.

Her arms filled with paper plates, napkins and cups, Melissa paused in the doorway before returning to the kitchen. Derek's back was to her, and he was looking toward the living room. With his coat off, his muscular build was impressive. If he'd gained any extra pounds in the eight years since he'd gone to work for her father, she couldn't see them. Nevertheless, he'd changed. Most noticeable were the symbols of his improved status. His pale blue shirt was silk, his pinstriped suit had been tailored to fit his extra broad shoulders and muscular legs and his shoes were the finest Italian leather. And the man looked comfortable in his clothes, wore them well. Derek Vincetti, the streetwise kid, had come a long way in eight years.

But Melissa knew the trip hadn't been without pain. At twenty-five, even though he'd had his share of knocks, he'd had eyes that were warm and an enthusiastic attitude. Last Christmas, at the office party, she'd been struck by how cold his dark brown eyes had become, how harsh the lines of his face and that he never smiled. With his Roman nose, high cheekbones and square jaw, he'd never been picture-book handsome, but she'd once loved to see him smile and to listen to his laughter. That night, last December, watching the way his wife treated him, Melissa knew who had changed him. It had hurt her to see Derek being humiliated in front of his coworkers, and she'd hated the tall and beautiful Carolyn Vincetti.

Now he was divorced—available—and in the same house with her. Perhaps it was time to find out why for eight years she compared every man she ever met to Derek. Why every man always came up short. Maybe it was time to get over a case of puppy love.

Or turn it into something more.

Chapter Two

Derek waited until the children were gone before he again issued his order. "Get your things, Missy. I'm taking you home."

"I am home, Vincetti," she said, sinking into an easy chair. Outside it had started to rain but the temperature hadn't dropped a degree, and the old air conditioner Gwenn had bought from a friend couldn't handle the heat Melissa had created while baking the pizzas. Pearly beads of moisture gathered on her forehead. She felt drained and wilted and in no mood for a battle. But she had no choice. "This is my home until I quit this job."

"Then you're quitting. Today. Now."

"She can't," gasped Gwenn, coming back from seeing the last child out the door. "She's needed here."

Derek turned and looked at the woman. He had no desire to disrupt anyone's plans, but he had to. "Missy's also needed at home. She's supposed to be getting married."

"Married?" Melissa repeated, the surprise in her tone bringing his attention back to her. "To whom?"

"Paul Thorton."

"Who told you that?"

"Your father." Derek had heard rumors around the plant, as well.

A shake of her head flipped her hair from side to side. "Paul asked, but I turned him down. Dad knew that. I like Paul as a friend, but that's all."

Derek lifted his eyebrows. He'd overheard Marge, Stanley Davenport's private secretary, tell Denise, the bookkeeper, that she'd walked into Davenport's office thinking it was empty only to find Missy and the Thorton guy in a passionate embrace.

"Don't give me that look, Vincetti." It was obvious he didn't believe her. "I have nothing against Paul, but he's too much like Dad." Both men were always trying to program her. "I think Dad and Paul's father see a marriage between Paul and me as a great way of merging Thorton Electronics with Davenport Computers. Which they can just forget. I'm not marrying a man just because it would be good for the business, especially not a man who thinks worrying about the environment is a phase I'll outgrow. And I'm not leaving here."

Derek frowned and stepped toward her, and Melissa's eyes widened. "Derek Vincetti, don't you dare do what you're thinking." Quickly she straightened in the chair and sat as tall as she could. Pointing a finger at him, she said the first thing that came into her mind. "You cannot carry me back to my father like a piece of luggage. Not this time. So stop acting like a Mafia hit man and sit down and we'll talk about this."

To her surprise, he did sit. With a frustrated snort, he planted himself on the edge of the couch and stared at her. And she wanted to laugh, if only to release the tension within her, but she didn't dare.

"So start talking," he said.

Gwenn spoke first. "Melissa, I've got that class tonight, but if you want me to stay, I'll call and cancel."

"No, that's not necessary." For Derek, she explained. "Gwenn teaches a university extension class in Newport."

"I teach how to teach reading skills," Gwenn said. "There's only this class and two more, so I hate to cancel, but if I'm going to be there on time, I've got to leave soon. Still . . ." She kept a wary eye on Derek. "I feel I should be here."

"Don't be silly," Melissa chastised lightly. Maybe she was being too hopeful, but she didn't think Derek would try kidnapping her. "I'll be here when you get back." She watched Gwenn head upstairs to change before turning back to Derek.

Derek had grown quite good at reading people. Body language told a lot. Missy's hands—the way she kept rubbing them together—said she wasn't feeling as confident as she sounded. She also kept licking her lips, and he wished she wouldn't. Watching the tip of her tongue slide over full, perfectly shaped lips was having a strange effect on him. He forced himself to look at her eyes.

They were almost brown today, and they sparkled with a determination that said she'd fight him all the way. She'd always had spunk, and he'd always liked that. Today she also had an air of assurance. Maybe she was worried about what he'd do, but she believed in herself, believed in what she was doing. He liked the woman she'd become. Not that liking her would stop him from doing his job. "You can't stay here, Missy. It's not safe."

"Of course it's safe. That little fight with the boys wasn't anything I couldn't have handled. Jim wasn't trying to hurt me."

"I'm not talking about those kids." Though he wondered if she truly understood the anger and resentment the one boy harbored within. He'd seen it in Jim's eyes and knew the feelings. Unless someone got to him, someday Jim would hurt someone.

Derek lowered his voice. "Missy, you're the only child of a very wealthy man. You're working with children from low-income families. How long before someone realizes you're a walking gold mine?"

"Meaning like before?" It had happened seventeen years ago, but she could still remember the terror she'd felt when John Fuller pulled her into his car and took her to an old abandoned house. Maybe if John had been a cruel man, the experience would have left her with deep-seated emotional scars, but John had treated her nicely, always apologizing, always saying he didn't want to hurt her, he just needed the money. No, Derek couldn't use her past to scare her. "If I let the fear of being kidnapped rule my life, I'd have to live in a fortress and never go out."

"You don't have to live in a fortress, but there are some places and situations you should avoid."

"And teaching here is one of them?" Melissa scoffed at the idea. "Try another, Vincetti. That argument won't hold water."

He shrugged. "All right. What about your father, your parents? Don't you owe them something?"

"I owe them a lot. I'll admit that. But it's also time for them to let me stand on my own two feet."

"Why don't you call your father? Talk to him?" Derek motioned toward the telephone by the stairs in the entryway. "If you convince him that you should stay, I'm out of here."

Out of here and out of her life. She wasn't sure she wanted that. Furthermore, she knew a call to her father would be a waste of time. "I can talk to Dad about the weather, about politics and about religion, but every time I try to talk to him about what I want to do with my life, we get into an argument. He thinks he can rule me—program me the way he does those computers of his. Well, I'm a person, not a machine."

Derek understood her problem. He doubted if any man loved a child more than Davenport loved his daughter, but the guy did like everything to proceed like a well-structured computer program. Melissa had a habit of becoming a glitch.

She sighed. "Really, Derek, I don't want to hurt my parents. I love them. But I can't be what they want and talking never helps. That's why I didn't tell them what I was doing. I knew this was how they'd react, that they'd send you after me."

Derek stood and walked over to the plate-glass window that faced the street. Outside it was growing darker, and the rain was coming down in a sheet, the wind whipping it against the car he'd rented at the airport. Absently he rubbed the back of his neck. He felt tired. Davenport had called him Tuesday and given the order that his daughter be found and brought back to California immediately. Since then Derek had made telephone calls, sent faxes and flown from San Francisco to Nashville. Missy had tried to cover her tracks and hide her whereabouts, but it didn't take him long to locate the right people in the right places. She was working for a school district. She'd had to fill out papers, file her credentials. It was amazing how easily a man dressed in an expensive suit could convince a clerk that he had the authority to look into confidential files.

The sound of someone coming down the stairs made him turn away from the window. Gwenn Bradley stood at the bottom step, looking at him. She'd changed from her tan slacks and muted green blouse to a white blouse, gray skirt and high heels. She'd been quite congenial when they first met; now she was frowning. He wondered how much of the argument he'd been having with Missy she'd overheard.

Finally Gwenn turned toward Melissa. "You sure you'll be all right?"

Melissa rose from her chair and walked over to the older woman. "I'll be fine. If Derek gets too ornery, I'll make him sit in the corner, like we do the kids."

Gwenn's gaze went to Derek. Again she glared at him, her expression stern. Then her posture softened, and she hugged Melissa. "I'll be back early."

After Gwenn left, Melissa faced Derek. They were alone, but she felt at a disadvantage. A day of working with hyperactive, troubled children had taken its toll. Flour spotted her blouse and slacks, and she was sure her makeup and hair were a mess. What she needed was time—time to work up a strategy to convince Derek to give up this idea of taking her back to California and time to create a better impression.

"I'm going to take a shower and change. While I'm upstairs, would you mind turning off that worthless air conditioner and opening a few windows where the rain won't blow in? I think that would be cooler than it is now. When I come down, I'll fix us some dinner." She didn't wait for his response but headed for the stairs. Before she went up, she paused. "I'd offer you a drink, but with the kids coming here, we don't dare keep any liquor in the house."

"I don't drink," Derek said. "And I'll take you out to dinner."

Melissa shook her head. She wasn't getting in a car with him. If she did, the next thing she knew—whether it was legal or not—he'd have her on a flight back to California. "It's too nasty out to drive anywhere else, and the best Red Oak has to offer is a coffee shop where everything oozes grease. I've got some chicken in the refrigerator. It won't take long to broil."

Derek watched her go up the stairs, each bouncing step she made swinging her hair against her shoulder blades. For all her new maturity, Missy didn't have the haughty air of sophistication so many of the women in her family's financial and social position took great pains to cultivate. Women like his ex-wife.

It was Carolyn's haughtiness that first attracted him to her. She'd had everything he thought he wanted: polish, sophistication and class. And, unbelievable as it was, she decided she wanted him, called him, invited him out...seduced him. And like a blinded fool, he'd congratulated himself on his good fortune.

Later he'd paid the price.

After Melissa disappeared from his view, Derek went over and turned off the rattling, antique excuse for an air conditioner, then opened the windows on the leeward side of the house. Immediately the air inside began to stir, making the heat more bearable. He could hear Missy's footsteps as she moved about upstairs, then the pipes groaned and he knew she'd turned on the shower. He wasn't afraid she'd sneak out on him. Missy Davenport was a fighter for causes, not a fugitive.

This cause was different from those in her past. Teaching troubled children to read and write seemed a lot more reasonable than when she'd chained herself to a tree to keep it from being cut down, or when she'd tried to live like a bag lady to see how it felt. Nevertheless, it looked as though she'd thrown herself into this project with the same vigor she'd approached her other causes.

Glancing around, Derek could see her contributions to the house's decor. Colorful wallpaper covered the kitchen walls; bright pillows, cheerful paintings and whimsical mobiles accented the functional, neutral-colored living room and dining room; and throughout the house there was a feeling of lightness and brightness. He couldn't imagine Gwenn Bradley, with her sedate wardrobe, choosing hot pinks, flaming oranges or iridescent blues. Missy would do that.

His chore completed, Derek sat down in the chair Melissa had occupied only a while earlier. Maybe he was imagining it, but he'd swear he could still smell her perfume. He'd noticed the light, airy scent earlier, when he first arrived. In the heat of the kitchen, it had been stronger, but never overpowering. Not like so many of the perfumes Carolyn had used.

For a moment Derek closed his eyes. His divorce was final now, but the decree had been nothing more than an affirmation of what he'd known—what both of them had known—soon after the wedding. His mistake was staying with Carolyn for three years, thinking things would change, that he could help her. If anything, his efforts to get her to stop drinking had made things worse. It had taken the Christmas party to make him face that.

The pipes in the walls banged as the water upstairs was turned off, and Derek opened his eyes and looked up at the ceiling. Melissa had been at that Christmas party, and he'd never noticed her, never seen how pretty she'd become. He never wanted to relive that night, but he did wish he'd taken a moment to pay attention to her. Just one moment.

With a sigh, he again closed his eyes.

Her feet bare, Melissa came down the stairs without making a sound. She wasn't trying to sneak around, but when she saw Derek asleep in the chair, she was glad she'd been quiet. There was something special about watching a man sleep. It was a time when he let down his defenses, relaxed. For the first time that day, Derek didn't look tense and on guard. There was even a slight upward curve to his lips. The man was almost smiling.

For a moment she stood at the bottom of the steps and stared at his mouth. She was tempted to cross the room and touch her lips to his. That would definitely give him a surprise—and her a thrill. She'd certainly spent enough hours as a teenager dreaming about what it would be like to kiss Derek Vincetti—and to have him kiss her back. She doubted reality would ever equal those childish daydreams.

The only thing kissing him would prove was that she was no more mature now than she'd been then. Which was why she turned and walked into the kitchen. As quietly as she could, she started dinner.

Soon the aroma of broiling chicken filled the house. Potatoes were baking in the microwave, and Melissa was tearing lettuce into bite-size pieces when she realized she was no longer alone. Looking over her shoulder, she saw Derek. He was leaning against the doorjamb, a lazy, sleepy look still softening his expression. Once again she had the urge to cross the room and give him a kiss. And once again she resisted the urge. "Welcome back from the land of nod, Vincetti. Dinner will be ready in about five minutes."

"I can't believe I fell asleep." He also couldn't believe he was really awake. The woman standing by the counter was a man's dream of paradise come true.

She'd used a blue-and-green cloth band to hold her hair back from her face and a few pins to secure its length in a loop. When she wore her hair up, he had a clear view of her neck. He also had a clear view of most of her body.

The blue-and-green halter she was wearing tied on top around her neck and on the bottom around her ribs, exposed every inch of her slender arms, most of her back, and all of her small, flat midriff. He knew by most standards that the halter was a perfectly acceptable piece of clothing, but the soft cotton accented the lush curves of her breasts and definitely left little to the imagination.

Her shorts weren't much better. They covered her tight little bottom, but they certainly showed a lot of leg. Lots of smooth, tanned, enticingly bare legs.

Quickly Derek looked back up at her face. "You've changed."

She was sure he didn't simply mean her clothes. Smiling, she turned completely round so he could really see how she looked. She'd worked hard to get this figure, and she wasn't against using it to her advantage. "I knew the kitchen would be hot, so I decided to put on something more comfortable."

Let me slip into something more comfortable. Derek had heard those words before, from women trying to arouse him sexually. *Is that what you're up to, Missy? Do you think you can use sex to distract me from doing my job?*

Again Derek let his eyes travel down her body. He didn't want to be aroused, but a man would have to be a monk not to be affected by this woman. He doubted even a monk would be immune to Missy's youthful sexuality. Pushing himself away from the door, he walked over to the sink and turned on the tap. What he needed was a glass of water—cold water—and to remember why he was here. "You know, your parents are worried about you, Missy."

"So tell them I'm fine." She moved to his side, her bare feet hardly making a sound on the linoleum. It had only been there for a moment, but she'd seen the look of desire in his eyes. Then he'd shut the emotion off, quickly and decisively. Only she didn't want him to ignore that feeling. Touching his arm, she said softly, "Missy was a plump, silly teenager, Derek. Please call me Melissa."

He glanced at her face, at her warm, inviting smile, then at the hand on his arm. Her long, slender fingers rested lightly on the dark hairs that covered his skin, and a tingle raced down his back. She wasn't as small as some women he knew, but there was a delicate quality about her. A vulnerability. Perhaps because she was so trusting, so sincere in her beliefs, he'd always felt protective toward her. Tonight he had a feeling he was the one who needed protecting. He was too experienced not to recognize a come-on.

Ignoring the surge of desire her touch triggered, he patted her hand. "If that's what you'd like, Melissa. Now, what about your father? When are you going to call him?"

"In time." Derek wasn't reacting as she'd hoped, and she wasn't sure what to do next. Once her mother had said a woman was born knowing how to attract a man, but Melissa didn't feel as if she knew what to do. Not now. Not with Derek.

The timer on the microwave went off, and she jumped—startled—then silently thanked Providence for an excuse to move away. "The potatoes are ready. Why don't you sit down? Dinner will be on the table in a minute."

He waited until her back was to him before he allowed himself to take a deep breath and savor the sweet, feminine smell that lingered in the air. She was apple-blossom shampoo and jasmine perfume. Innocence and temptation. Considering the way she was dressed and how long it had been since he'd been with a woman, he congratulated himself on managing to keep his hands off her. Nevertheless, his body had reacted, and he was glad she'd kept her gaze on his face.

Over dinner they talked—about the weather, about his flight, and about the differences in the landscape between Tennessee and California. They were skirting the more important issues. He knew it, and she knew it. Finally he asked about her job.

Melissa was a little surprised by the question. "Knowing how you work, and all the information you're always able to gather on anything I get involved with, I figured you'd be familiar with everything about this job by now."

He finished his third piece of chicken, wiped his hands on a napkin and leaned back in his chair. "Let's pretend I know nothing. You tell me why you're here."

"So you can explain to my father why I'm staying?" She wanted to emphasize the point that she didn't plan on going back with him.

"You'll have to explain that to him yourself. I'd just like to know why for my own curiosity."

"You want to know why I'm doing this?" she repeated, then rose and refilled his glass of iced tea, taking the time to organize her thoughts. No matter what he said, she knew he would relay her answer to her parents. That was his job. "Well, first you have to understand this area. Most of the people who live in

Red Oak have had very little education. The majority didn't finish high school. Some farm, some do mountain crafts and sell them to tourists, and some drive to Pigeon Forge and Gatlinburg and work in the restaurants and motels during the tourist season."

Derek gave a cynical snort. "The ones I talked to must never leave town, if you can call that place a town. I asked one man where the school was, and he stared at my suit like he'd never seen one before. And an old man came out of the grocery store with an old woman, took one look at me and jerked the woman back into the store as if I might gun them down or something."

Melissa laughed lightly. She could imagine what the townspeople had thought when they saw Derek. Seeing his suit and sophisticated looks, they were probably afraid he was a revenue man. "Don't forget, these are people who used to make white lightning in stills hidden in the woods. Some probably still do. They're a little suspicious of strangers, and not exactly in sync with the modern world."

"Which you're going to change, of course."

"We're at least going to teach their children how to read and write, and give the younger ones a better start in school. A lot of these kids are caught in a cycle of ignorance and poverty. We hope by working with them here on a one-to-one basis—by working with kids like the boy who was in the fight today, by teaching someone like Jim that there are other ways to do things than what he's learned from his parents and neighbors—we can break that cycle."

She looked at Derek. Over the years her father had told her bits about his background. His home life hadn't been all that different from Jim Allerton's. "What made the difference with you, Vincetti? Why are you wearing a designer-label suit today? What got you off the streets?"

His answer was simple. "Sergeant Hull."

"Sergeant Hull?" She didn't understand.

Derek took a long drink of tea before he answered. "When I was fourteen, Gordon Hull caught me trying to rob a store. Instead of arresting me, he gave me a lecture and took me home to my dad. And from that day on, he was like a big brother, always dropping by, taking me places and talking to me. And when my dad died during my senior year in high school, Sergeant Hull moved me into his house, and I discovered not everyone lived the way my family had, that there was another way."

"Which is exactly what we're trying to do here," Melissa said enthusiastically. "That's the purpose of the Learning House. We want to show these kids another way. We want them to see a home that's different from what they're used to. See magazines and newspapers on a coffee table, books on shelves. Hear different types of music. Eat different types of food."

"Like pizza?" He smiled.

It was the first time she'd seen him smile since he'd arrived, and she loved what it did to his face. And to his eyes. The coldness was gone, replaced by a warmth she could bask in. "Believe it or not, that was a different experience for them. And I even got a little math into the process."

"Speaking of math, I saw what you're making on this job. You got more from your dad for an allowance when you were in high school."

"And spent it on foolish things, most of which I didn't need. The cost of living isn't as high here as it is in Silicon Valley. I'm satisfied with what I'm making."

"Does Gwenn know how much you're worth?"

Melissa hesitated. "I guess so, more or less. She knows I wouldn't have to work if I didn't want to, and that my father's the founder and president of Davenport Computers."

"Have you been bragging about that to anyone else around here?"

His curt tone irritated her. "I wasn't bragging when I told Gwenn. She needed to know I wouldn't desert her in a month or two for a better-paying job."

"You didn't answer my question." And he needed to know. "Have you told anyone else that you're worth millions?"

Melissa snorted. "I'm not worth millions, Derek, my father is. And no, I haven't been running up and down the streets saying, 'Look at me, I'm rich, I'm rich.'"

He narrowed his eyes, his dark brows coming closer together. "Not funny, Missy."

"It's Melissa. Remember?" She hated being patronized. "I'm not a child. I know better than to go around bragging about the money my parents have. Don't be so paranoid."

"Being cautious is not being paranoid. You were kidnapped once. Your father's afraid it might happen again."

"No, my father's looking for an excuse to get me back home. Any excuse. I am perfectly safe here. Stick round for a while and you'll see that."

Chapter Three

Almost since his arrival, Melissa had been trying to think of a way to get Derek to stay in Red Oak, at least for a while. If she was going to investigate this attraction she'd felt for so long, she needed him around, and since she didn't want to go back to California—not yet—the only alternative was for him to stay in Tennessee. "You know, Derek, you could spend some time here. You could use Rob's room."

"Rob's room?" Derek's eyebrows shot up.

"Gwenn's son. This last summer he often stayed here. Besides visiting with his mom, he helped us renovate this old house, so we've gotten in the habit of referring to the extra bedroom as his. But Rob's at college now. So why don't you stay here? See what I'm doing. Get to know the area and the people. I guarantee when you go back to California you'll tell my folks I'm as safe here as I would be there."

She wanted the idea to sound casual. Spontaneous. If he knew how just a smile of his turned her insides upside down, he'd use that to his advantage. Hoping he wouldn't realize how nervous she was, Melissa rose and began to clear the table. "Well, what do you think?"

Derek watched her carry their dirty plates to the sink. There was no missing the tension in her body. "You want me to stay here, in this house, with you?"

"And Gwenn," she added quickly. "Gwenn has one bedroom upstairs, I have another and you'd have the third. It would be perfectly proper."

He wasn't sure if in Tennessee a man living with two women was considered proper or not, especially when the one scooting around in front of him looked so tantalizing in a halter and shorts, but the idea did have appeal. Lately he'd wanted some time away from work to sort through his thoughts, consider his options and make plans for his future. He could do that in Red Oak and still keep an eye on Missy. "Just exactly how long are you suggesting I stay here?"

"I don't know." For a lifetime sounded good. "A couple of weeks. Maybe a month."

"And then you'd go back without a fuss?"

Melissa stopped picking up their dirtied utensils. She'd started viewing Derek's presence as a chance to get to know him, a chance for him to get to know her. He hadn't forgotten his job.

Well, she had a job, too. "I'm not going back with you, not unless you plan on staying until next summer."

Derek stood abruptly, his quick action pushing his chair back so it wobbled and nearly fell. His voice was low pitched, stern and unyielding. "Oh, yes, you are!"

He towered over her, and there was no way she could fight a man of his size or hope to win a battle of strength. They both knew that. They both also knew there was no way he could force her to go with him, not legally. Melissa straightened, tilted her head back so she was looking him squarely in the eyes and boldly restated her position. "No, I'm not. Dad may think what I'm doing here is crazy or that I'm in some great danger, and you may have orders to bring me back, but this time you're going to have to tell him I said no."

"If I remember correctly, you said the same thing six years ago, that night I found you at Reverend Sanjo's house, ready to give yourself to him."

"I was not ready to give myself to him, and you know that. All I had planned to do was live in the house for a while, then write a story for the papers." Naively she'd thought her "I was there" story would bring in tons of money and create more safe houses for runaways. At seventeen, she'd had dreams of her literary work receiving a Nobel or Pulitzer Prize. Or at least praise from her father. "I thought Reverend Sanjo was really just letting those girls stay at the house because he was concerned about their welfare. I had no idea once you shared his food you also had to share his bed. Besides, that has nothing to do with what I'm doing now."

Derek knew she was right, but he was tempted to pick her up and sling her over his shoulder as he'd done that night six years ago. How much easier it would be if she were still underage and he could simply carry her out of here and back to her father. Viewing Missy as an adult wasn't comfortable. He didn't like the thoughts that kept slipping into his head. The woman should have more clothes on, shouldn't look so tempting.

She was only inches away, and it would be easy for him to reach out and touch her, see if her skin felt as velvety smooth as it looked. Easy and dumb. He turned and walked out of the kitchen.

Melissa watched him go into the living room. Once again she'd seen that look in his eyes, the look of desire. And maybe her mother was right, maybe a woman did know what to do. Melissa knew she couldn't let Derek get away. She set the utensils back down on the table and followed him.

He was standing in front of the plate-glass window, looking out at the street. Darkness had settled over the quiet neighborhood, and the pelting rain had driven even the local cats and dogs under shelter. No cars traveled the shiny, wet pavement, and lights in living rooms showed most families were watching television. The only things of interest within Derek's view were the puddles rapidly forming on the sidewalk and lawn, and the brown van parked halfway down the street.

He appeared totally absorbed by the scene.

Melissa paused for a moment to stare at his imposing profile. Like the storm outside, he could be fierce and frightening, but she'd seen him gentle, knew how tender and kind he could be. It was up to her to weather this squall. She had to stay in control, had to come up with the right words, the right tone. If not, he'd leave, and she'd lose her chance to be more than just the boss's daughter to him.

"I know you feel an obligation to my father to bring me back," she said, once again moving toward him.

Derek glanced over his shoulder, his eyes dark, hooded and wary.

"And maybe my lying to my parents about having to stay with a sick friend seems immature, but I had to do it. When I first read about this job, I knew I had to come here, had to talk to Gwenn and see if this was what I wanted."

"And is it?"

His was a precise, decisive question. She couldn't be that sure. "I think so, but I really haven't had enough time to find out. This summer we fixed up this house and ordered supplies. I've only been working with the kids for a little over three weeks."

"And how long did you think you could keep up your story of a sick friend?"

She shrugged. He'd turned to face her, and she wished his gaze weren't so intense or his posture so intimidating. It was difficult not to slip back into the role of a bumbling teenager, especially considering how little thought she'd given the matter of her excuse to her father. "I don't know. It was coincidence that Julie called right after I'd read Gwenn's ad in the NEA bulletin. The idea of saying Julie was sick and needed me just popped into my head. I figured Dad wouldn't question my flying east to be with her. And he didn't. Then, after I came here to Tennessee and Gwenn offered me the job, I had to come up with a reason not to fly back to California."

"So you kept on telling your dad Julie was sick."

"Yes." His gaze was accusing, but Melissa refused to look away. "I know it doesn't sound like I planned this endeavor any better than I planned any of the other things you've been sent to rescue me from, but believe me, this is different. Gwenn is no kook, and I'm in no danger here. I'd have told Mom and Dad what I was doing if I'd thought it would help. But they just won't listen to me. They have their own ideas of what I should do with my life, and you can't believe the pressure they put on me."

She sighed in frustration. It would be easier if her parents were abusive or if she hated them, but neither was true. Her parents simply believed that what they wanted for her was best. And they insisted on it.

So, to make it easier on herself—and on them—she'd told lies and put thousands of miles between them. She couldn't go back, not yet. Not until she was sure this was what she wanted.

Melissa moved closer to Derek. "So what do you think, Vincetti? Will you stay for a while? Will you give me a chance to prove that this time Stanley Davenport's crazy, airhead daughter knows what she's doing?"

Looking into eyes that were now almost a dark green, Derek had no doubt Melissa knew what she was doing. She was using her sex appeal to get him to let her stay. Using it very effectively.

It was no airhead standing toe-to-toe with him. The low, seductive pitch of her voice was well thought out. As well planned as her choice of attire and the beguiling scent of her perfume. What Stanley Davenport's little girl was doing was fighting dirty.

She'd been shy around him as a teenager. Back then if he smiled at her, she'd blush. Now it was *her* smile that had him flustered, and with her tempting body so close, he was the one who wasn't sure where to look.

Or where to put his hands.

He locked them behind his back.

"Well?" Melissa repeated, her voice almost a purr.

"Well, what?"

His growl didn't fool her. She knew he was uncomfortable with her standing so close. He might have clasped his hands behind his back, but hers were free. Slowly, teasingly she ran the tips of her fingers over the triangle of tanned skin and dark hair exposed by his shirt's open collar. "Will you stay for a while?"

She felt muscles tense beneath her fingertips, but his words gave no indication that what she was doing bothered him. "And how would my staying help? My job is to take you back to your father. You, on the other hand, keep insisting you're not going back. What difference will a few days make?"

Maybe no difference, but she wanted to find out. Melissa dropped her hand to her side, turned away and walked toward the dining room. The children had cleaned up before they left, but two sports magazines lay on the table, left by one of the boys. She picked them up.

It was time to bargain. Time for a compromise. If she wanted him to stay, she was going to have to take a chance. Carrying the magazines back to the coffee table in the living room, she considered one possibility. When she faced Derek, she stated her proposition.

"Stay a month, Vincetti. Live here, in this house, with Gwenn and me. Watch what we're doing, what I'm doing, and if at the end of that month you still feel this is a harebrained idea and I'm in danger, I'll go back with you."

"I can't stay here for a month, Missy." He at least liked to think he was needed back at the plant.

"Three weeks."

He shook his head.

"All right, make it two weeks." That would be better than nothing, and she was quite certain by the end of that time he'd agree with her that living in Red Oak, Tennessee, was a heck of a lot safer than living anywhere in California.

He watched her straighten the magazines on the coffee table, then go over and fluff the pillows on the couch. Her suggestion wasn't a bad one. He wouldn't mind spending a couple of weeks here, and it would be nice if Melissa would go back with him willingly. Peacefully. With her being over twenty-one and here of her own free will, he couldn't very easily drag her back to Daddy just because that was the way Davenport wanted it. And while he was here, he could keep an eye on her and check out the area. If she wasn't in any danger, he could report that to Davenport, and who knew, maybe her father would change his mind about wanting her to leave.

Melissa knew Derek would look at all sides of her proposition. That was his way. Fussing with the pillows, she gave him time to think, but after a while, she faced him. "Well?"

"I haven't decided."

At least it wasn't an out-and-out no. She was pleased with that. Careful not to let a grin give away her pleasure, she headed for the kitchen. "Take your time, but while you're making up your mind, I'm going to do the dishes."

Melissa was scrubbing the broiler when Derek came into the kitchen. With her heart lodged in her throat, she stopped washing and turned to face him. "Well, what did you decide?"

"That I'll give you my answer tomorrow."

He was dragging it out, torturing her, and Melissa wondered if that wasn't part of his strategy. Knowing him, she assumed he probably hoped she'd get worried and give in or make more concessions. Well, she wouldn't. She figured her proposition was a sure thing, that after spending two weeks with her, Derek would see there was no reason to take her back to her father. Her gamble was he'd also see she was more than the boss's daughter, more than a problem to be dealt with and handled efficiently.

All she could do was wait and see. "As soon as I'm finished here, I'll show you Rob's room."

Grabbing the dish towel hanging by the refrigerator, Derek picked up a glass from the drain rack. "I'll help."

Surprise dropped her mouth open, then brought laughter. "Derek Vincetti wiping dishes? I don't believe it. Heavens, what would the men at the plant say if they heard about this? Listening to them talk about you last Christmas, I'd have thought you were Silicon Valley's answer to Rambo."

"What did they say?"

He'd stopped wiping, his expression tense and guarded. Melissa knew he was aware that some of the comments made about him the night of the party had included references to his wife. She wasn't ready to bring up the subject of Carolyn Bronson Vincetti. Not yet.

Grinning mischievously, Melissa went back to washing the broiler. "Well, let's see. I heard you single-handedly rescued one of the secretaries from the bathroom when the door stuck."

He relaxed and chuckled. "A man's got to do what a man's got to do."

"And—" She'd truly been impressed by some of the stories told that night. "I heard you discovered a spy working at the plant."

"Oh, that guy last fall. It was nothing big time," he assured her. "Just an amateur who thought he could make a little extra cash by letting your dad's competitors know what was being developed at Davenport's. He got sloppy, and I got lucky."

The way she'd heard it, it wasn't luck but Derek's keen perception that first keyed him in to the fact that something wasn't quite right. And then it was his stealth and persistence that brought in the necessary evidence. "I heard when Dad confronted the guy, Mr. Spy tried to make a run for it, and you had to chase him down and subdue him."

"That's my job. It's what your dad pays me to do."

"He's gotten so he calls you Rambo, too." That hadn't bothered her, but she hadn't liked her father calling Derek the Italian Stallion. She refused to think about why that irritated her. "I don't know what he'd do if you weren't around."

She handed him the rinsed broiler.

His hands covered hers, his fingers holding hers captive against the metal, his voice soft. "And now you want to keep me away for two weeks?"

Looking up into his dark brown eyes, she smiled. "Yes."

He followed her up the stairs, his eyes locked on the wiggle of her bottom as she took the steps two at a time. Her shorts were a decent length; it was his mind that kept thinking indecent thoughts. The idea of spending two weeks with Missy was ridiculous. He had to be crazy even to be considering it.

"This is my room." At the top of the stairs, she pointed to her right. There were four doorways along the hallway, two on each side. "And this is Gwenn's." Her hand moved to indicate the room opposite hers. "Bathroom's next on the left and the room on the right will be yours."

She led him to that room and opened the door. A wave of heat hit them, but the room had a clean, cheerful appearance. It would be better than a lot of rooms he'd stayed in.

"I don't know what you brought with you, but I think Rob left a razor and some toilet articles, plus a few clothes in the closet."

She glanced at him, then laughed, her dimples showing. "Forget the clothes. Your shoulders are twice the size of Rob's, and you've got about six inches on him in height. Even if you could get into his jeans, they'd come up to your knees."

"Don't worry about the clothes. I brought a change, and if I stay, I'll buy what I need."

Derek moved about the room, investigating his surroundings. Both curiosity and caution were parts of his nature. The mismatched furnishings and rug were old, but the blue-and-green patterned wallpaper, painted trim and tie-dyed bedspread and curtains looked new. In the closet he found two pair of jeans and three T-shirts. A bottle of after-shave sat on the dresser. It was a cheap brand that was popular with teenagers. He'd used it years ago.

The bed was a single. Derek tried it with his hand, and it squeaked a little but was firm. It would do. Walking over to the window, he pushed back a curtain and looked down on a pair of peach trees, a swing set and a picnic table.

"You'll want to open that," Melissa said. Beads of sweat had already started to form on her brow. The room felt like an oven.

Going to the window, she nudged Derek aside, unlatched the lock and, with a grunt, strained to push it up. "Since we painted it, it sometimes sticks."

"Here, let me." He positioned himself behind her, placed his hands beside hers and pushed.

The window easily slid up, and Melissa's arms were stretched above her head. A gust of cooler air hit her bare belly, and she sucked in a breath and backed up.

Her shoulders hit Derek's chest, her bottom his hips. He hadn't moved back.

Quickly she shifted forward again, laughing to cover her embarrassment. "You make it seem so easy."

It had been, and now that the window was open, he wondered if she hadn't played weak just to get him close. The touch of her body had excited him, then she'd pulled away. But she hadn't moved far, and the breeze cooling his body also carried whiffs of her perfume, of her shampoo and of her sweet, womanly scent. She was tempting him again, teasing.

And a man could only stand so much teasing.

Derek's hands dropped to her bare shoulders, and he turned her so she faced him. "Just what are you trying to prove, Missy?"

"Me?" They were no closer than they'd been earlier in the living room, but this was different. Her back was to a window, and she had no easy escape. Derek didn't look nervous or flustered. The glint in his eyes was decidedly dangerous. "I'm not trying to prove anything."

"Sure." Slowly Derek trailed a fingertip down the side of her throat to the top of her halter. His gaze rested on the rapid rise and fall of her breasts. "If you wanted me to realize you've changed, you've succeeded."

That had been exactly what Melissa had wanted, but suddenly she wondered if it had been such a good idea, or if she'd changed at all. As he ran the fingertip down her arm, his light touch sent shivers over her skin. He was igniting a fire deep within her. Missy the teenager had blushed every time this man had smiled. Well, Melissa the adult now had the flushed cheeks, and it was an effort for her to speak. "I—I don't know what you mean."

"I think you do." He smiled knowingly, and his hand moved to her waist. Slowly he traced the bottom edge of her halter with his fingers, his wrist lightly brushing against the underside of her breasts. "What I'm wondering is how far you're willing to go to keep me from taking you home."

"How far I'll . . ." Melissa's eyes widened as she realized what Derek was saying, then she stiffened under the hand on her shoulder and glared at him.

Much as she liked Derek, she wasn't ready to jump into bed with him. Damn the man! Why couldn't he understand that all she wanted was for him to see she was no longer a child? Angry, she tried to move away. "If you mean will I sleep with you, the answer is, you're crazy, Vincetti."

"Am I?" He stopped her escape by quickly shifting his hands to her waist and pulling her to him. Her hips came into contact with his and her breasts pressed against his chest. "Then why the skimpy attire?"

"It's hot." And getting hotter by the minute. Rain-cooled air hit her backside, but the heat of his body and the look in his eyes had her steaming.

"And the invitation to stay with you?"

"Stay with Gwenn and me. In your own room. By yourself. All I want is for you to see I don't need rescuing."

"So you're not interested in me as a man? Not at all?"

She hesitated. Though she was not opposed to a lie or two when necessary, lying wasn't a basic part of her nature. Still, this time it did seem a necessity. "Not at all."

He might have believed her if her heart wasn't racing like an overrevved engine. Or if she'd looked him in the eyes. But she'd looked away.

He wasn't sure what game she was playing, but he knew he liked the feel of her in his arms. It had been a long time since holding a woman had aroused him, but he was aroused now. And he knew she could feel it. They could say whatever they wanted, but their bodies were communicating on a more basic level, a more honest level.

"So you don't want me to kiss you?" Derek asked, his voice softer. Gently he drew her up on her toes.

She looked at him again, her eyes locking on his mouth. Melissa knew she should say no, but she couldn't answer. For eight years she'd dreamed of kissing this man. For eight years she'd wondered if reality could even come close to fantasy.

Her silence gave him his answer. Lowering his head, he brushed his lips over hers.

Melissa sucked in a breath. She wanted more, not just a teaser. She had uncles who kissed longer than that. Her hands went to Derek's shoulders, stopping him from pulling back. Although she felt as frightened and excited as a child about to take her first ride on a roller coaster, Melissa closed her eyes and pulled his head toward hers.

Again Derek's mouth touched hers.

This time his lips stayed on hers, and he kissed her, truly kissed her. And Melissa knew why none of the boys she'd ever dated had been able to convince her that they were the one she wanted to give herself to; why no man had ever made her forget the dark-haired half-Italian with his piercing brown eyes.

One kiss, and Melissa knew reality could be as good as fantasy, that dreams could come true.

Derek's hands roamed over her back, keeping her close, while his lips moved over hers, nibbling and tasting. Claiming. Making her his. She was riding that roller coaster, holding on for dear life, afraid to let go, afraid to open her eyes. Never had she felt such exhilaration, such excitement.

And then the ride came to a screeching halt.

Swearing under his breath, Derek loosened his hold and pulled back.

A few hours with Missy Davenport, and he was acting like a young stud. He wasn't thinking, at least not with the right part of his anatomy. Because if he had been thinking, he would have remembered this was not the type of woman he wanted to get involved with. Once should have been enough to teach him fancy clothes and a few dollars in the bank didn't put him in the same league Missy Davenport and Carolyn Bronson played in.

Opening her eyes, Melissa stared up at a frowning face that clearly stated Derek wasn't happy with what he'd just done. In true Davenport fashion, when faced with opposition, she got angry. "Let me go!"

He didn't. "No. We still have some things to discuss."

"Like what?" At the moment, all she wanted was time alone. Time to lick her wounds. Kissing Derek had been heaven for her; from his expression, she'd rate his reaction as a quick trip to hell.

"We need to discuss your behavior if I decide to stay."

"*My* behavior?" Waggling a finger under his nose, she lashed out at him. "*My* behavior's just fine, buddy. *You're* the one with a problem, coming into this house like a bounty hunter ready to carry me off. I'm offering you a chance to face this situation reasonably. I'm giving you an opportunity to stay here as an observer, so you can go back to your employer—my father—and tell him his little girl is quite capable of living her own life, that I'm safe and sound. But no, you go and misunderstand everything, go and kiss me. Then you have the audacity to question *my* behavior."

She ran out of breath or she would have gone on. He simply stared at her.

And then he began to laugh.

Chapter Four

The next morning the memory of Derek's laughter still brought a flush of color to Melissa's cheeks. His kiss had sent her emotions soaring, his laughter had hit her like a slap to the face.

He would never know how much willpower it took not to turn tail and run. All night as she tossed and turned in her bed, she'd applauded herself for smiling sweetly, then slowly walking away. All night she'd also questioned her sanity.

Why want a man who treated her like a child? A man who could take a kiss that had seemed so right and turn it into mockery? She had to be insane to want him around for two weeks—a real masochist to think those dark eyes would ever look at her with respect. With passion. With love.

Physical exercise was the best way Melissa knew to banish a case of embarrassment. As she did every weekday morning, she went down the stairs before the sun rose, pushed the coffee table in the living room to the side and slipped a videotape into the VCR. A few leg stretches took her through the usual FBI warning at the start, and she was warmed up and ready by the time the exercise routine began.

No one would know the jabbing motions she made with her arms were punches directed at Derek's face. And only she knew what part of his anatomy was benefiting from her kicks. Her ponytail slapped against her back and perspiration trickled down her forehead, only to be stopped by a bright pink sweatband. Breathing hard and fast, she put heart and soul into her kicks and jabs, determined to exorcise the demon haunting her.

Derek wasn't sure what the noise was he heard coming from downstairs. He wasn't even sure why he was up, other than that his head ached. It was a too-much-tension, too-little-sleep type of headache, and he remembered seeing a bottle of painkiller in the cabinet by the kitchen sink.

At the top of the stairs he paused, automatically tensing. The voice coming from below wasn't Missy's—the tone was too strident. And it wasn't Gwenn's. There was no trace of Gwenn's soft Tennessee drawl.

Years of security work made him wary. Slowly, soundless, he crept down the stairs. Whatever was going on, the woman was counting. "One...two...three..."

Breathlessly counting.

By the time he reached the bottom step, Derek was smiling. The thumping and heavy breathing had taken on meaning. Silently positioning himself by the living room doorway, he watched Melissa kick her legs into the air.

Pink tights and a fluorescent pink-and-yellow striped leotard hugged her body like a second skin. Her face was flushed, her eyes riveted on a spot somewhere in front of her. She was totally oblivious to his presence, and he knew he should say something, at least make a sound so she'd know he was there.

He didn't.

Nature had been kind to Melissa Davenport, and had given her long, graceful legs and a body to match. The once-pudgy teenager had slimmed down to a streamlined combination of angles and curves. Full, firm breasts bounced temptingly with each kick, and he remembered how good they'd felt pressed against his chest.

Over the past eight hours, he'd remembered a lot of things about Missy—the feel of her, smell of her. Taste of her. Kissing Melissa Davenport had been a mistake. He'd responded to her, reacted without thinking. That had been stupid. She was the boss's daughter.

And she turned him on.

He'd laughed at the way she got all incensed when he mentioned her behavior. What a spitfire. What irony. Here he'd been sent to protect Missy from the bad guys. Well, who was going to protect her from him?

Or him from her?

She wanted him to stay for two weeks. Could he and not touch the forbidden fruit? Could he resist what was out of his league?

He hoped so because he really hadn't come up with any other idea to get her back to California. For most of the night he'd tried to think of ways. All he'd ended up with was a headache. Derek rubbed his temples.

Something alerted Melissa that she was no longer alone. Stopping almost midstep, she spun around and faced the doorway. Derek was leaning against the wall, massaging his head with his fingers. He was naked to the waist, the thick mat of dark hairs covering his chest narrowing to a ridge that disappeared under his belt. Barefoot, his dark hair rumpled and his eyes only half opened, he looked disheveled, bemused and sexy as all get-out.

Any anger that remained after her exercise vanished. No matter how Derek viewed her, she couldn't stop the way he made her feel. Like it or not, she adored the man.

"Good morning." With her forearm, she wiped the perspiration from her face. "You're up earlier than I expected."

"I'm up earlier than *I* expected. I was looking for something for a headache." His gaze darted to her leotard. She wasn't wearing a bra, her nipples making pointed impressions beneath the stretchy material. Just as rapidly he looked away. "You do believe in bright colors, don't you?"

She glanced at her outfit, then back at him. If she wasn't mistaken, he looked uncomfortable. "I guess I do." The exercise tape played on, but Melissa ignored it. "Let's take care of that headache. What do you want, aspirin, non-aspirin, or ibuprofin?"

"Whatever's easiest."

She walked past him, toward the kitchen. Her skin had a shiny glow, and her breathing was still uneven. She was acting as though nothing had happened the night before. He was glad. He wasn't up to dealing with recriminations or an emotional tantrum.

Melissa opened one cupboard. A bottle of small tablets sat beside a box of bandages. "Down here we have the non-aspirin, for the kids. Gwenn keeps the others upstairs. I rarely have a headache."

He hadn't had a headache since he'd left Carolyn. He should probably view this one as a warning. "Whatever you have's fine."

Melissa handed him the bottle and drew a glass of cold water from the tap. "Sit down—" She nodded toward the table. "I'll rub your neck and shoulders."

Derek glanced at the chair. A neck rub would be nice, but considering the way he'd reacted last night—was reacting this morning—he didn't dare let her touch him. A woman wearing a skin-tight leotard and smelling delightfully feminine was just too enticing. He shook his head and quickly popped two pills into his mouth, then downed them with water.

Melissa was certain she knew why he'd refused her offer. "Darn it all, Vincetti, I am not trying to seduce you."

"Did I say you were?"

"It's what you were thinking." She'd bet anything.

Looking down at her, he lifted dark eyebrows. "I didn't realize you were a mind reader."

She wished she were. Or maybe she was better off not knowing what went on in his head. "You made it perfectly clear last night what you thought."

"About last night—"

"Forget last night." She wished she could. "If you don't need anything else, I'm going upstairs to take a shower. Gwenn will be getting up soon. We usually have breakfast at seven, then get ready for the kids. If you want to go back to bed, we'll try to keep it quiet, but I make no promises."

"I'm not going back to bed." Sleep was not what he wanted. And what he did want, he couldn't have. Shouldn't have. "Where do you keep the coffee?"

"Cupboard near the stove. Top shelf," she instructed, then quickly asked, "Derek, did you think about my proposition?"

"I did." For most of the night.

"And?"

"I haven't decided."

At nine o'clock fifteen pre-kindergarten children came bouncing, jumping, yelling and crying through the door, and Derek knew it was a good time to get out of the house. He told Melissa he wanted to look around, check out the area. She was busy helping a tearful little girl take off her jacket and only nodded. Gwenn was quieting the rest of the children. He didn't bother saying anything to her.

There were twelve houses on Missy's street—five plus the school on her side of the road, seven on the opposite side. It was as close to a subdivision as the town of Red Oak offered, the houses all about forty years old, two story and designed like cracker boxes. Stanley Davenport would be glad to hear his daughter wasn't living in a slum, as he'd feared. Knowing Missy, Derek had been prepared for anything.

The town of Red Oak wasn't very large, its population 996 according to a sign posted at the edge of town. As far as he could tell, that number had to include cats and dogs.

The central business district took up two blocks. There was a gas station, a grocery store, a newspaper office, a library, a hardware and the coffee shop Missy had mentioned. There were also several souvenir shops with signs advertising native mountain crafts. All had Closed signs on their doors.

He drove out of town. The countryside was hilly, and the narrow road to the south wound its way up a steep mountain slope, past houses and trailers, small farms and dense stands of timber. The rain from the night before had washed away the oppressive mugginess and clouds, and a clear, blue sky formed the backdrop for the Great Smokies.

He'd never spent much time in the mountains. City boys whose fathers drank themselves to death didn't get to go hunting or camping. He'd been lucky to get out of San Jose and discover Muir Woods. And though he'd been up to Lake Tahoe a few times since taking the job at Davenport Computers, those trips had been few and far between, especially after he married Carolyn. Travel was not one of his ex-wife's passions.

Derek checked his watch. It was nine-thirty. Davenport always rose at seven during the work week. Subtracting the three-hour time difference, he had a half an hour until it would be time to call the man and let him know he'd found his daughter. Meanwhile he could use another cup of coffee.

Turning the car around, Derek headed back down the mountainside. He liked the quiet, easygoing feel of the area. The beauty. Every dip and bend in the road presented picturesque views—green fields contrasted to red earth, lofty pines, rocky bluffs and meandering streams. An old man ambled from a trailer set back on a small section of land. Slowly he headed toward the mailbox by the side of the road, a dog of dubious ancestry waddling along beside him. Neither was in any hurry.

Time seemed to have stopped in this section of the country. It was like taking a step into the past. Red Oak was a far cry from the fast-paced, congested city Derek had left three days before. Here a man could take stock of himself, could look around and see where he was. Could think about where he was going.

The coffee shop in Red Oak was nearly empty, and the girl at the cash register told him to sit wherever he liked. As Derek headed for a booth near the window, he realized the waitress and others were watching his every move. Considering that the three men at the counter were dressed in blue jeans, bib overalls, and work pants, Derek could understand why a navy pinstripe business suit made it obvious he was an outsider. If he did stay, he'd certainly have to modify his wardrobe.

If he stayed.

Davenport wouldn't want him staying. Tuesday afternoon he'd made it clear he expected Derek to find Missy and bring her straight home. Derek supposed he should feel pleased that Davenport placed such confidence in him. The man hadn't even suggested Derek might not find Missy or might have problems getting her to come home. But then, that was because Stanley Davenport still thought of his daughter as a child. Last night, Derek had discovered Missy was anything but a child.

He still wasn't sure what happened in that bedroom. One minute he was chastising her, trying to make her see what she was doing, the next he was kissing her. And with that one kiss, he knew he was in trouble. She'd felt so perfect in his arms, responded so willingly, aroused him so quickly. He'd had to do something.

Take her to bed.

Laugh.

She'd been angry as all get-out. Defiant.

Adorable.

If he had a brain in his head, he'd figure a way to get Melissa Davenport back to California. And fast.

"Coffee, honey?" the waitress asked in a sweet, Southern drawl.

Derek looked up, startled. He'd forgotten where he was. "Yes, please."

"You're not from these parts, are ya?"

"No."

Carefully she poured his coffee. "Just passin' through or are ya plannin' on stayin' awhile?"

"Just passing through...I think." Hoped. "Is there a telephone around here I can use?"

The waitress shook her head. "One we got ain't worked in a nearly a month. They keep sayin' they'll get it fixed, but they don't. There's one over there, by the newspaper office." She pointed out the window and down the street. Nearly hidden by a tree was a pay phone mounted on the wall of a white wooden building. "Last I knowed, it still worked."

"Thanks."

"Ya welcome, honey. Y'all decided what you want for breakfast?"

He lifted the cup. "Just coffee."

"Then y'all have a good day." She smiled and moved on, checking if the men at the counter wanted refills of their coffee.

Derek sipped his and stared across the street at the newspaper office and its lone, hopefully working, telephone. He wasn't looking forward to making this call. Stanley Davenport wasn't going to understand his daughter's refusal to come home. Or like her proposition.

Nevertheless, Derek couldn't see any way to force her to leave. Or any reason. Nothing he'd learned about the project she was involved in and nothing he'd seen, not even the scuffle he'd interrupted the afternoon before, indicated she was in any danger.

Of course he could be mistaken, and maybe he should stick around for a couple of weeks, as she'd suggested. Then he'd have a better picture of the situation and could give Davenport a more thorough report. Only staying around Missy for a couple of weeks wasn't really a wise idea. Not for him, at least.

At ten o'clock, Derek paid his bill and headed across the street to the phone. Determined to get the ordeal over, he punched in Davenport's number, then the number of his credit card and waited. Davenport's maid answered on the third ring. Two minutes later, Stanley Davenport was on the line. Derek's report was straightforward and simple.

"I found her."

"Is she all right?"

"She's fine."

"When will you be bringing her back?"

"That's a problem." Derek cleared his throat, knowing what he was about to say would cause an explosion. "She doesn't want to come back, and I don't see how I can force her to."

Davenport's response was about what Derek had expected, and for a few minutes he let the older man sputter and swear. It wasn't until Davenport suggested he tell Missy that her mother was dying that Derek broke in. "I don't think she'd believe that, sir."

"Well, you can't let her stay there. It's not safe."

"As far as I can tell, sir, she's in no danger. She says no one except the woman she works for knows how much she's worth. Around here, I doubt if anyone's even heard of Davenport Computers, much less connected Missy to the company. I know you and your wife are worried about her being kidnapped again, but I don't think there's any danger of that."

Davenport merely grumbled.

"I really think you should talk to her yourself, sir. I copied down the telephone number at the house where she's living. Wait until this evening, after she's finished working with the children. If you call at four o'clock your time, I'll make sure she's at the house."

Just the slightest sound behind Derek caught his attention. Quickly he turned. Near the doorway to the newspaper office stood a middle-aged woman with gray-streaked brown hair and wire-rim glasses. She smiled, then gestured toward the phone. She wanted to use it. Derek wondered how long she'd been standing behind him, and how much she'd overheard.

"I've got to hang up, sir," he said, turning his attention back to Davenport. "If you talk Missy into coming home, I'll have her on the next flight out of here. If not, she did make one suggestion you might consider."

Derek gave the man a moment to consider his options, then lowered his voice. Succinctly he relayed Missy's proposition, ending with the pros and cons. "It means I'd be away from the plant for two weeks, but it might give us an edge. She said if I can prove she's in any sort of danger, she'll come back with me without a fuss. And one thing I know about your daughter, if she gives her word, she'll stick to it. So what do you think?"

Stanley Davenport's answer was simple. "I think you'll find a way to get her home."

Chapter Five

Derek didn't return to the Learning House until five-thirty. Melissa saw him park his rental car in the driveway, watched him grab his coat and a bag of groceries from the back seat, and waited as he strolled leisurely up the sidewalk. Heart in her throat, her stomach in knots, she opened the door; he stepped in as casually and confidently as if he owned the place.

She'd been on edge all day, wondering where he'd gone, when he'd return and what he would do when he did return. Physically and emotionally drained, she snapped at him like a shrew. "Where have you been?"

"Here and there." Derek looked around. Missy had changed from slacks and a top to a multicolored, tie-dyed skirt and blouse and sandals. She looked tense, but the house was quiet. "Kids all gone?"

"They left half an hour ago."

"And Gwenn?"

"Upstairs in her room, getting ready for a date."

His dark eyebrows rose. "A dinner date?"

"Yes." Her gaze dropped to the bag of groceries in his arms. "What's that for?"

"Dinner, but I guess Gwenn can have her steak another night."

"Dinner?" Here she'd been worried that he'd be upset when he came back and learned they'd be alone, had been afraid he'd accuse her of once again trying to seduce him. He, on the other hand, was simply taking over her life. "How do you know I don't have something planned for dinner?"

"Do you?"

She didn't. She hadn't known what to plan. "Maybe."

He grinned. "Does it sound better than a thick, juicy steak? I just thought as long as I'd moved in on you guys, I should supply dinner."

Irritation switched to hope. "Does that mean you're staying?"

The telephone rang. Melissa ignored it, waiting for his answer, but Derek looked away, first at the clock on the living room wall, then at the telephone. Again it rang. "Aren't you going to get that?" he asked.

She supposed she had to.

The telephone was on a wooden crate that had been set up-end and painted a bright enamel blue. From its position by the stairs, anyone using the phone could see into the living room, the dining room and parts of the kitchen. When they were working with children, being able to see what was going on was important. As she lifted the receiver, Melissa kept her gaze on Derek.

Her hello was automatic, then she listened to the voice on the other end of the line. In a moment, she called up to Gwenn. "It's for you. It's Bill."

Derek shifted the sack in his arms and started for the kitchen. "I'm going to take care of these groceries. If we're not going to eat them, they should be refrigerated."

Melissa laid the receiver on the crate for Gwenn to get, then followed him. "You didn't answer my question."

"What question?" he asked, keeping his back to her. Item by item, he began emptying the grocery sack.

"Are you staying?"

"Tonight? Yes."

"And for the next two weeks?"

Derek set a bag of potatoes on the counter, then turned to face her. "I promise I'll tell you that later."

"How much later?"

He smiled. That was all, just a smile, yet Melissa couldn't stop the sudden acceleration of her heart. No man's eyes should be that sexy, no smile that compelling. She wanted to reach up and touch his chin, feel the rough stubble where a day's growth of beard had become a dark shadow, run her fingertips over his lips and know the whisper of his breath.

Her own breath came out a husky whisper. "So I just have to wait?"

"I..." Derek's words trailed off, and he stared deep into her eyes. Then suddenly he shook his head, like a dog shaking off water. Or a man getting rid of a wayward thought.

Once again he turned back to the bag of groceries. "I'll tell you later," he repeated. "So what's your decision about dinner? Steaks or..."

The steaks did look good, and he'd bought all the fixings to go with them. "As long as you went to this much bother, let's have the steaks. Do you want me to cook them?"

"I can do it. One thing I've learned over the years is how to cook." Derek glanced her way. "You've had a busy day. Relax."

With him around? That was impossible, but she did lean back against the counter. "Did you stop at Mark's Market in town?"

"No, Kroger's in Knoxville."

"How did you like Knoxville?"

"It was okay. Typical city." He lifted a bottle from the bag. "Since I don't drink, I bought this. I hope it's all right. If you want wine..."

Sparkling water was fine with her. "I don't need wine."

He unscrewed the top, his shoulder muscles bunching beneath the soft cotton of his white shirt. His clothes smelled of fresh air and sunshine, and his shoes were scuffed and dusty. One thing for certain, he hadn't spent the entire day in the city.

There was an effervescent hiss. "Glasses?" he asked.

Melissa found two champagne glasses on the top shelf of the cupboard by the sink and rinsed them off. Derek filled each halfway, then handed one to her. Raising his, he offered a toast. "To Tennessee and the Great Smoky Mountains."

"To Tennessee," she repeated and took a drink.

The water was cool and bubbly, tingling as it ran down her throat. She grinned and ran the tip of her tongue over her lips. Derek watched, then reached out and touched where her tongue had passed.

He'd built a reputation as being a tough guy, but the look in his eyes was tender and the stroke of his finger as gentle as a feather. Melissa waited, her heart beating wildly. Ever so slightly, she leaned toward him.

It was at that moment when Gwenn barged into the kitchen. "Well, it looks like I'll be eating dinner at home after all. Bill's—"

Melissa straightened, and Derek jerked back his hand. Both looked at Gwenn, and her gaze darted from Derek's face to Melissa's, then back to his. Quickly Gwenn changed her tone. "Maybe, on the other hand, I'll go into Knoxville."

"No. Stay and eat with us," commanded Derek. *Protect me from myself,* he silently added. He couldn't believe he'd touched Melissa again. Thought of kissing her. Where was his willpower? Quickly he turned back to face the counter.

Gwenn stared at them, and Melissa shrugged. She certainly couldn't explain what was going on. One minute she thought Derek was going to kiss her, the next he treated her like poison. "What happened with Bill?"

"A sick child. His ex called him and asked him to pick up a prescription. To tell you the truth, I don't think the man's ready for a relationship. Last time we were out, all he did was talk about his ex and his kids."

"Are you looking for a relationship?" asked Derek. He pulled another glass from the cupboard.

"No, not really. My work here is going to take most of my energy for a year or two. Maybe longer. If the Learning House works in Red Oak, we want to try it in other districts where there's a high dropout rate."

Derek poured her some of the sparkling water, then handed her the glass. "Here's to the Learning House."

Gwenn took a sip, her gaze shifting between Derek and Melissa, then she grinned. "Melissa was concerned when you were gone so long today. She was afraid you might have gotten lost."

He cocked an eyebrow at Melissa. "You should know I don't get lost."

"I'm not sure I know you at all." He certainly had her guessing now. "I thought you were sent here to rescue me. Isn't that rather difficult to do if you're nowhere around?"

"Oh, I've been around." Setting his glass back on the counter, Derek picked up a potato and turned on the water. "I did a little investigating today."

He would have, of course. "Have you checked out all of Red Oak's bad guys? That shouldn't have taken long." Melissa laughed wryly and headed for the refrigerator. If she was right, they still had some sour cream left, and she loved sour cream on baked potatoes. "Don't you ever get tired of playing errand boy for my father?"

"Yes."

His blunt answer surprised her, and she stopped and looked back.

"I also get tired of getting you out of trouble."

"I haven't been getting myself into trouble."

"She's right," Gwenn said. "In the three months I've known her, Melissa hasn't gotten into any trouble... unless you consider accepting two dates for the same night trouble."

Immediately Derek stiffened. "You've been dating?"

His incredulous attitude irked her. "Some men do find me attractive."

The potatoes forgotten, he faced her. "Who have you been dating? What do you know about them?"

"What do I know about them? Come off it, Derek. You're starting to sound like my father."

He snorted, his dark eyes delving deep into hers, and she lifted her chin and stared back. If he were jealous, that would be an encouraging sign, but she had a feeling Derek's proprietary attitude was simply an indication that he didn't trust her to pick a proper mate.

It was Gwenn who again spoke up in her defense. "Mr. Vincetti... Derek, I can assure you that Melissa's dates have all been upstanding citizens. Should I make a salad?"

His gaze never left Melissa's face. "If you like."

Gwenn moved between them, and Melissa took the opportunity to turn away from Derek, back to the refrigerator. He made another disgruntled sound, and she grinned and found the container she'd been looking for. Let him fuss and fume. She could handle that. And she could handle her father. She realized that now. She might just call him later, after everyone had gone to bed. It would still be early in California. She'd put off talking to her parents long enough. If she couldn't stand up to them now, she'd never be ready.

Derek resumed scrubbing the potatoes, and Melissa carried the sour cream over to where he had the rest of the food. He'd rolled up the sleeves of his shirt, and when he reached for another potato, his bare arm brushed against hers. Immediately he jerked his hand back, as if pricked by a pin, and his reaction irritated her. "I don't bite."

He grunted.

"You sound like a caveman. Your entire attitude is prehistoric. Tell me, Vincetti, do you run a security check on every woman you take out?"

"It's different with me."

"Why, because you're a man?"

"Because I'm not worth millions."

"In other words, a man would only be interested in me for my money?"

"That's not what I said."

"What are you saying?" she demanded.

"That you're too trusting. Too naive."

"I'd rather be naive and trusting than a cynic." Melissa turned and walked out of the kitchen.

As Derek baked the potatoes in the microwave, broiled the steaks and prepared the salad dressing to go on the salad Gwenn was putting together, Melissa set the table in the dining room. She felt more comfortable away from him. Near him, she was either a basket case or bristling. Life wasn't fair. The two men she'd dated since taking this job had been nice, considerate gentlemen. So did they make her heart race or her knees go weak? No. She had to be enamored with a Neanderthal. A cynical Neanderthal.

It wasn't until they were eating that Derek actually told them what he'd done during the day. "I drove around this area most of the morning, getting to know where each road led. I ended up in Sevierville."

"Did you go on to Pigeon Forge and Gatlinburg?" asked Gwenn.

"I drove through Pigeon Forge." He slabbed some butter onto his potato and mashed it in. "Quite the tourist trap."

"Did you go to the theme park?" Melissa couldn't imagine him there, but she knew several people who thought the place was great.

"No." Derek glanced at his watch. "I'm not here on vacation."

"Going somewhere?" She pointed to her bare wrist, tapping the spot where he wore his gold watch.

For a second he looked like the cat caught with the canary, then he quickly shook his head. "No."

"Forgetting Pigeon Forge," continued Gwenn, "what do you think of the area?"

Derek looked back at her and answered. "Beautiful country. I would love to have time to go into the park."

Would love to. Melissa knew those were the key words. If he didn't have time to visit the Great Smoky Mountains National Park, that meant he wasn't planning on staying.

Staring at the steak on her plate, she had a feeling that this was her last supper, and Derek was her Judas. She wanted to ask how he planned to get her back to California, yet she knew she'd be wasting her breath. He wouldn't tell her. It would just happen.

"Have you always lived around here?" he asked Gwenn.

"Not actually around Red Oak; I just moved here in June. But I've lived in Tennessee all my life. I grew up near Nashville and went to college in Knoxville. I got my teaching credential there."

"What does one have to do to get a teaching credential in Tennessee?"

Melissa only half listened as Gwenn told him. College courses and teaching credentials weren't what she wanted to discuss. How to stay in Tennessee was her problem. But when Derek mentioned his bachelor's degree in business, Melissa did interrupt. "I didn't know you went to college." She'd always thought of him as the streetwise kid who'd barely made it through high school.

"One reason I wanted the job at Davenport Computers was the college plan. I couldn't have afforded to go to school if the company hadn't picked up the tab."

The telephone rang, and Derek tensed. Melissa could actually see the muscles in his arms flex and tighten. On the second ring, he looked directly at her. "Aren't you going to get that?"

"I'll get it," said Gwenn and pushed her chair back.

"No, let her." It wasn't a suggestion; it was an order.

Melissa knew then why he'd been checking his watch. He'd been expecting this call. And as she rose from her chair and walked over to the phone by the stairs, she knew exactly who the caller was.

"Hello, Daddy," she answered.

Chapter Six

Derek watched her talk into the telephone. He couldn't catch all she was saying, but he could follow enough of the conversation to know Stanley Davenport wasn't convincing his daughter to come home. Melissa's inflexible posture practically shouted her anger, and the looks she cast his way made him want to duck for cover. Derek cringed when she slammed down the receiver. For a moment she stood where she was, staring at him, then she turned and headed straight for the front door.

It banged shut behind her like a shot on a battlefield. He didn't move, didn't speak. Didn't breathe. He was trapped between his duty as an employee and his feelings as a man.

Gwenn was the one who summed up the moment. "Boy, is she mad at you."

"With good reason, I suppose."

"You were expecting the call?"

"Yes."

"You gave her father this number?"

"Yes."

The phone rang again, and this time Gwenn answered it. After a second, she held out the receiver to Derek. "It's for you."

"Stay with her the two weeks she wants. Keep an eye on her and keep her safe, then bring her home." Those were Stanley Davenport's orders. And Derek Vincetti was Davenport's errand boy. He hated it, but at the moment he had no alternative. Leaving the house, he went looking for Melissa.

Her colorful tie-dyed skirt and blouse, its circles of red-orange, yellow, blue and green made her easy to spot. She was halfway down the block, nearly to the school yard, walking slowly, her shoulders slumped. Derek braced himself for battle and started after her, his steps far more decisive than he felt inside.

As he drew close, he knew she'd heard his footsteps. Her shoulders straightened and her head came up, her golden-brown hair falling in waves down her back. She didn't look his way, and she increased her pace, which suited him fine. He didn't want to stop and start arguing in front of one of the houses. What they had to discuss was private—personal.

Slowing his steps, he followed her.

Davenport didn't know what he was asking. Derek considered himself a man with strong willpower, but it wasn't going to be easy to remain cool and detached around Melissa. Not for two weeks.

Suddenly she stopped, spun around and faced him. "You're a cad, that's what you are. A snake in the grass."

He pulled up short, managing not to run into her, and held back a grin. Over the years he'd been called a lot worse than a snake or a cad. But there was no denying her anger. The streetlight above showed her eyes more green than brown. A stormy green, clouded and turbulent.

"Let's not talk here," he said. "It's too public."

"Afraid to let people know what you're up to?" She was too upset to care who saw or heard them.

"We'll talk there." Taking her by the elbow, he steered her toward the school grounds.

"Let me go! Dammit, Derek, I will not let you push me around like a child!"

She struggled to get loose from his grasp, but he held her securely and picked up his pace, maneuvering her toward the shadows of the nearest building.

"I'll yell for help," she warned, raising her voice and looking around to see if anyone might hear her. "I'll—"

"You won't do a thing. Not unless you want to embarrass yourself and Gwenn."

The mention of Gwenn's name was enough to lower Melissa's tone. She didn't care about herself, but she wouldn't drag Gwenn or the Learning House into her personal problems. More in control, she faced Derek. "You called him today, didn't you? Gave him my number. Even dinner tonight, that was to make sure I'd be there, wasn't it?"

"You had to talk to him," Derek answered and let go of her arm. They were far enough away from the nearest house to avoid being overheard, and the school building would shield them from prying eyes.

"I would have called him."

"When? Next spring?"

"I'd decided to call him tonight." She straightened her skirt and flexed the arm he'd held, surprised he'd had such control with so little pressure. Then defiantly she shook her hair across her shoulders.

"Sure." He scoffed and used his body to inch her closer to the wall. "What kind of daughter tells her parents lies and refuses to let them know where she is?"

"A daughter tired of having her life planned for her." Derek moved even closer, and she put up her hands, using her palms against the front of his shirt to stop him. She'd retreated far enough. "I'm not going back, not yet. And I don't care what Daddy says, you can't make me go."

The heat of her hands burned through the cotton of his shirt, stirring emotions that had nothing to do with his job or protecting Missy. Against his better judgment, he followed his orders. "I'm not going to make you do anything, but you offered me a deal last night. You said if after two weeks I felt you were in danger here, you'd come back with me. Willingly."

"I'm in no danger." Except for the way he made her feel. The rapid beat of his heart matched the crazy acceleration of her pulse.

"You don't know that for certain." He tried to keep her safety in mind and ignore the way his body was reacting. "I'm staying, Missy."

"Call me Melissa," she demanded.

"All right. I'm staying, Melissa."

"And?" She felt more in control, and slowly let her hands move up the front of his shirt to his collar.

"And—" he repeated, just a slight catch in his voice giving away the jolt of awareness the movement of her fingers caused. "I'm going to keep an eye on you."

"Good."

Her hands slid around his neck, her fingers combing into his hair, and he knew she was wrong, it wasn't good. He'd programmed electronic and computerized systems to respond to intrusions. His system was giving off warnings that he was in danger, that Missy was intruding on his emotions in ways he couldn't control. It was time to step back, break the contact and take a breather.

Derek didn't move.

"Then we have a deal?" she asked.

His breath came out a shudder. "Deal."

"Seal it with a kiss."

Melissa slid her hands higher, her fingers pressing against the back of his head, bending him to her. It was her body that touched his as she rose to her toes. She was the one who sought and found his mouth, her lips that moved over his and her pride she was putting in danger. If he laughed again, she'd die a thousand deaths and bury her feelings forever. If he pushed her away, she'd know she didn't have a chance.

But he didn't laugh, and he didn't push her away, and with a groan of surrender, he returned her kiss, his arms going around her, drawing her closer. Every agonizing hour she'd spent that day was suddenly worthwhile, every terrible thought she'd held against him forgotten. He was kissing her with a hunger she understood and shared, moving his hands over her back with the same fervor as her hands moving through his hair. Eight years of wanting were in that kiss. Eight years of dreams and frustrations. She yearned to hold on to the moment forever, only what was happening between them was too fiery to be held. Violently he pulled back his head.

"Don't toy with me, Missy."

"I'm not toying with you." But she was frightened. If he ever guessed the power he could wield over her, she'd be on the next plane to California.

His body was rigid, his physical need a real thing. "You're playing with fire, Missy."

She trembled in his arms but didn't pull away. "I'm not playing."

"This is crazy." Derek groaned, never loosening his hold.

"Totally," Melissa agreed. It was crazy that the stars above looked like diamonds on velvet, that the night creatures in the bushes were singing love songs, and that Derek's body should fit so well against hers.

"You're the boss's daughter." He couldn't clear that from his thoughts.

"I'm Melissa Davenport, a woman who teaches children with special needs." And she had a special need. Him. "Are you afraid of my father?"

"Afraid?" He tested the word. As a boy he'd been afraid of his father. As a man he'd learned to avoid danger and respect power. Stanley Davenport represented power. One word from the man and Derek Vincetti would be out of a job.

Which really might not be so bad.

Still, at the moment he was employed by Davenport Computers and on an assignment, and he was a man who believed in fulfilling his obligations. "No, I'm not afraid of your father, but I promised him I'd make sure you were all right."

Melissa rubbed her hands over the back of his shirt. The soft cotton gave beneath her fingers, while his body felt solid, strong and warm. Strength of body. Strength of character. Two very good qualities. She dropped the pitch of her voice to a sultry low. "And am I all right?"

In his opinion, she was perfectly all right, but not necessarily in the way her father was thinking. "That's what I'm going to find out in the next two weeks, isn't it?" he answered.

She certainly hoped so.

Saturday morning, Melissa knew what Derek had been doing all day Friday. He'd been busy sabotaging her anonymity. And he'd certainly done it in a grand manner.

"Why not just hang a price tag on me, Vincetti? Put a sign on my back? 'Here she is. Take her.'" She waved the Saturday edition of the Red Oak *Gazette* in front of his face. "You yell at me about telling Gwenn my family's rich! At least I didn't go to the papers."

Derek stared at the thin newspaper she dropped on the table. It was smaller in overall dimension than the *San Francisco Chronicle* or *San Jose Mercury News,* only a few pages thick and printed on poor-quality newsprint, but the headlines were certainly big and bold. "Heiress Residing In Red Oak."

Quickly he looked up at Missy. "I didn't go to any newspaper."

"Then how did they find out about me? About my connection to Davenport Computers? How did they know my father wants me home but I won't go? You're the only one around here besides Gwenn who knows that, and Gwenn certainly didn't tell Mary Sue."

"Who's Mary Sue?"

"The *Gazette*'s one and only reporter." Every wonderful, silly, romantic thought she'd had about Derek was gone. He'd played her for the fool, double-crossed her every time she turned her back. He was right—she was too trusting, too naive. She'd promised to go back with him if he proved she'd be in any sort of danger by staying. Now there was an element of danger.

But she wasn't going to play his game.

She wasn't leaving.

"It won't work, Derek. Maybe you've let everyone around here know my family's got money and that I was kidnapped when I was a child, but that doesn't mean someone's going to snatch me off the street here."

Derek scanned the article. He knew he'd never talked to any reporter, but it certainly looked as though he had. This Mary Sue had written that he was in town to bring Melissa Davenport back to her father, that Melissa didn't want to go and that he had two weeks to convince her otherwise. There were also references to the kidnapping seventeen years before. Everything was fairly accurate. What he did take exception to was the reporter's description of him as a character from the gangster movie, *The Godfather.* Some people were hung up on stereotypes.

If he'd been of a more malicious mind, leaking this story would have been a great idea. Or a stupid one. Pointing Missy out as a potential victim for a kidnapping was a lot like putting candy in front of a group of hungry children. As poor as the economy was around Red Oak, someone was bound to take a bite. He certainly wasn't going to take a chance on it. "We've got to leave now."

"We? Maybe *you* do. *I* don't."

Standing abruptly, the chair falling over as he did, he took hold of her shoulders. She felt so small. So vulnerable.

With a jerk back, she twisted out of his grasp. "Keep your hands off me!"

Stubborn could be added to his list of adjectives. And furious. If looks could kill, he'd be dead. "You don't understand the danger."

"No, you're the one who doesn't understand." She shook a finger at him, her face flushed with anger. Only a slight quaver in her voice gave any indication that she feared what he might do next. "This is my job; Red Oak is where I live. I am not leaving."

Shaking inside, she turned away and started for the door. Derek called after her. "Don't forget last night."

Melissa stopped and took in a deep breath, but she didn't look at him. How could she forget last night? The feel of his lips, the taste of him, smell of him...it was all branded in her memory. But he'd betrayed her, stabbed her in the back, and she also couldn't forget that.

"We have a deal," he insisted, his words firm and unyielding.

Slowly she turned.

"Two weeks." He stood tall and rigid, his dark eyes never wavering from her face. "If I prove you're in danger, you go back with me."

"But you've got to prove it," she said, wishing she'd never offered the proposition. "Prove, with a capital P. None of this, 'I think someone might try something.' It has to be a real threat to my safety. And no hiring someone to fake something."

"I wouldn't do that."

She wasn't completely sure. Her gaze moved to the paper on the table. He noticed. "I didn't talk to that reporter. I don't know how she found out about you, but it wasn't from me."

"Well, then, that's the first thing you need to check out, isn't it?"

It didn't take Derek long to discover who'd leaked the information about Melissa to the newspaper. The moment he stepped into the *Gazette*'s office and saw the middle-aged woman with the streaks of gray in her brown hair and wire-rim glasses, he knew he was looking at Mary Sue. He also knew she'd been standing behind him the day before a lot longer than he'd realized. And that she was a fairly good reporter, no matter how small this newspaper was. She'd taken what he'd said to Davenport, done some research, resurrected the story about Missy's kidnapping and had come up with a fairly accurate summary of what was going on. But admiring the woman's skills didn't lessen his irritation.

"What are you trying to do, put a woman's life in danger?" he demanded, dropping Melissa's copy of the newspaper on the reporter's desk.

Mary Sue had followed his progress from the door to her desk. He'd seen a flicker of fear in her eyes as he neared, but she'd suppressed it quickly, pushed her glasses up on the bridge of her nose and smiled at him. Now she stiffened in her chair, and the smile disappeared. "I report the news. That's all."

"You eavesdrop, that's what you do." And he hadn't watched his hindside close enough. He was getting sloppy in his old age. It wouldn't happen again. "Do you realize what you've done?"

Her smile returned, smug and self satisfied. "I've given our readers some very interesting news about the new teacher in town. That's what I've done."

"No, what you've done is set her up so any Tom, Dick or Harry who needs some cash is going to think a father who paid once for his daughter's safety will pay again."

Mary Sue scoffed at the idea. "Don't be ridiculous, Mr.—?"

He didn't supply his name. "Am I?"

"People around here don't kidnap others."

"I certainly hope not." Frustrated, he wished he could do more, give the woman a shake, break her computer or go back in time to the moment he called Davenport and Mary Sue came up behind him. Never again would he use an open telephone station for confidential information.

Controlling his anger, he turned and headed for the door. Before he reached it, Mary Sue called after him. "Did her father convince her to go home?"

Derek paused and looked back at the woman. Gone was her satisfied grin, replaced with a look of concern.

"I have a niece who's in the program," she continued. "Carrie really likes Miss Davenport. I'd hate to see her leave."

He stared at her for a moment, then shook his head. "You should have thought of that before you wrote that article."

From the newspaper office he drove to Knoxville and bought three pairs of jeans, three short-sleeved shirts, and three long-sleeved flannel shirts, a pair of hiking boots, a pair of running shoes and a polyester jacket. He'd seen the looks people had been giving him and knew that in a suit he stood out like a sore thumb. He was sure wearing what the locals wore wouldn't instantly eliminate their curiosity or suspicions, but he hoped it would help.

After paying for his purchases, he ducked into a restroom and changed, then made a telephone call to California. He didn't tell Davenport about the newspaper article; the man was already upset. Derek did suggest Melissa might be influenced by a visit from her mother or father.

It was interesting, neither was willing to fly out and talk to her face-to-face. Interpersonal communication was obviously not a Davenport forte. So Derek promised to call every night and report how things were going.

He also called and extended the rental of his car, then stopped at a station and gassed up. It was after noon when he pulled up in front of the Learning House.

The first thing he noticed was the van parked across the street. The same van had been parked down the street Thursday, and it had bothered him then. Unlike the typical family van, this one had no windows on the side panels, and the two small windows on the back doors were blacked out. Because it was a nondescript brown, Derek surmised it was a surveillance vehicle. Someone could have known Missy's identity long before this morning's newspaper article, might have already been keeping an eye on the house—on her.

And he'd gone and left her alone.

Derek slipped out of his car and crossed the street, his senses suddenly very alert and his body as tensed as if he were a soldier walking through a minefield. He forced himself to keep a casual pace, but he was ready for anything, his heart in his throat and his pulse pounding in his ears.

Slowly he passed the van, listening for sounds within.

He heard nothing.

He stopped, walked back, glanced up and down the street, then peeked in through the front windshield.

A heavy black curtain blocked the rear section of the van from his view. What he did see twisted his gut and sent a cold shiver down his spine. Lying across the passenger's seat was a gun case—an empty gun case.

Derek's gaze darted to the Learning House. Everything looked calm and quiet, but looks could be deceiving.

For a moment he stood where he was, considering a variety of plans of entry and immediately discarding most. One thing he knew for certain, if there was someone—or more than one person—inside holding Gwenn and Missy hostage, walking up to the front door would be foolhardy. His best bet was to go in through the back.

Quickly Derek crossed the street and worked his way around to the back of the house. Crouched low, he tried the rear door. It was unlocked. Cautiously he opened it and noiselessly slipped inside.

He was in the room where Melissa and Gwenn stored their extra supplies and did their laundry. The door to the kitchen was closed, but through it he could hear Gwenn and Melissa talking. Pressing himself against the wall, Derek listened.

"Trust me, I know where it is," said Melissa. And the next thing Derek knew, the door to the storeroom was opening.

She saw him the same time he reached for her. Her cry of surprise was immediately muffled by his hand over her mouth. She tried to pull away, but he drew her close, pushed the door shut with his foot and whispered in her ear. "How many of them are there?"

"Derek, what . . . ?" she cried the moment he lifted his hand from her mouth.

Immediately he clamped his hand over her mouth again, his orders brief and hushed. "I want you to get out of here. Get as far away from this house as you can and keep out of sight until it's safe."

He pushed her toward the back door, but she took no more than two steps then stopped, turned and faced him. "Derek Vincetti, what is going on?"

She certainly wasn't trying to keep her voice down. Nor was she following orders. Unsure when the others would come looking for her, he stayed near the door to the kitchen, but waved his hand toward the outside door. "Go. Get out of here. Let me take care of this."

He heard the telephone ring. Gwenn yelled, "I'll get it!"

That he hadn't heard any other voices was beginning to bother Derek. Either these men knew he was out here and were silently sneaking up on him, or he'd made a big mistake.

Missy stood where she was, shaking her head. "Now what? Is the mob about to blow me away? Or have aliens landed?"

"This isn't funny," he growled but relaxed a little. Even as stubborn as Missy was, he really didn't think she'd stand around and taunt him if she were in danger. "Are there men in there?"

"No. Should there be?"

Yes—no. He didn't know what to answer. "There's a van parked across the street. A very suspicious-looking van. And I saw an empty gun case on the front seat."

She grinned and stepped toward him. "And assumed we were being held hostage."

He felt like a fool. "It was a possibility."

"And was this a brown van?"

She stood right in front of him and looked up, her green-brown eyes sparkling with laughter, the dimples in her cheeks winking at him. For a moment Derek tried to maintain some semblance of dignity, then he chuckled. "Yes."

"It belongs to the Martins, who live down the street. Tina uses it when she goes to clean someone's house. She keeps her vacuum and cleaning supplies in the back. "But maybe you're right." She laughed lightly. "Maybe I should be worried. Tina might vacuum me away."

"It's not parked down the street, it's parked right across from this house, with an empty gun case on the front seat. Does this Tina clean house with a rifle?"

Melissa shrugged and walked over to the shelves along the far wall and began looking in boxes. "No, but Tina's husband Jack is a hunter. And Mike, who lives across the street is a hunter. Around here, hunters have guns. And sometimes they do take them out of their cases. Ah, there it is." She pulled out a jar of gold glitter.

Gwenn swung open the door, not even seeing Derek as she stepped past. "Melissa, that was Edith on the phone. She said she saw a man sneaking around the house. Do you think I should call the police?"

"No, don't worry about it." Melissa grinned and motioned to where Derek stood. "It was my bodyguard. He's going to save us from Tina and Jack Martin."

"From Tina and Jack?" Gwenn turned and faced Derek. "Why? What have they done?"

He gave her a sheepish grin. "Nothing. My mistake." Derek had a feeling it was going to take a while before he lived this one down. The past twenty-four hours he'd been making quite a few mistakes.

The doorbell rang, and Gwenn went to answer it. "Busy place," said Derek, following Melissa into the kitchen.

"Maybe Edith called the police herself. I don't know why you're so worried about my safety. She keeps a sharp eye on everything that goes on around here. You weren't out of the house more than ten minutes yesterday, and she was over here asking about you."

"You have a visitor, Melissa," Gwenn called from the living room. "Jim wants to talk to you."

"Jim?" repeated Derek, bothered by the instant surge of jealousy that filled him.

He followed her into the living room, ready to find fault with any man who'd come to call. When he saw the awkward teenager standing by the front door, Derek relaxed and slowed his steps, letting Melissa go on ahead. Jim Allerton looked as uneasy about this visit as he might a trip to the dentist.

"Ah, Miz Davenport, I, ah—" His gaze switched to Derek, and Jim nervously shifted his weight from one foot to the other.

"Don't worry about him. Just pretend he's not here." Melissa was glad to see the boy. Of all the afterschool students, Jim worried her the most. He had the potential to do well in school, but he always seemed so rebellious, and there was absolutely no support from his father. That Jim had come to the house on a Saturday was a complete surprise. "What can I do for you?"

"Ah—" Jim looked directly at Melissa and blurted out his message. "You, ah, once said you'd like to know more about coon huntin'. Well, me and my pa are gonna take the dogs out tonight, jest to see how a new one we got runs. Pa said for me to ask you ta come along."

"Tonight?" It was awfully short notice, and she didn't like the idea of hunting for raccoons, but she knew it was a way of life for a lot of the men in the area, and she had told Jim she was interested. She'd thought it would help if they had something besides school and homework to talk about.

"Yeah, Pa said tonight was a perfect night to do it."

Considering how hostile Jim's father was to the idea of his son being sent to the Learning House, Melissa felt she had no choice. This would give her a chance to talk to the man, hopefully get him to understand what they were doing. She really couldn't refuse to go. "Sure, sounds good."

"Really?" Jim looked relieved and backed toward the door.

"What time?"

"Around dark. Pa said to tell you he'd pick you up, and for Mrs. Bradley not to expect you until late. Real late."

Once again Jim looked at Derek, then his gaze came back to Melissa. Staring at her pink jump suit and sandals, he frowned. "Y'all'd better wear some different clothes than them. And some better shoes. Boots, if you've got 'em."

Chapter Seven

"I'm going with you." Derek made his announcement the moment the boy left the house.

Melissa looked at him and shook her head. She knew why he wanted to come. It wasn't because he yearned to spend an evening in the great outdoors. Nor was he looking for an excuse to be with her. No, he'd be by her side to protect her—from the bogeyman or some other danger he'd dream up. The man was paranoid. Eight years of working for her father had twisted his brain.

It was really a shame.

Slowly she walked toward him. Blue jeans and a cotton T-shirt looked good on the man, gave him a rugged, untamed appearance. Earlier in the back room, when he'd pulled her close and clamped his hand over her mouth, she'd been afraid. She'd felt the power in those muscular arms and known she was in danger. Gazing at him now, she knew she was still in danger. As much as she wanted to stay angry with Derek, she couldn't stop the way he made her feel inside.

Love was a ridiculous emotion. How could she love a man who was plotting against her happiness? Who took orders from her father?

She'd rather blame the giddy sensation in her stomach on the flu, only up until ten minutes ago she'd felt perfectly fine. Until Derek had grabbed her in the back room, her heartbeat had been steady and her breathing normal. Now she could hear her pulse in her ears, and the closer she drew to him, the more she wanted to reach out and touch him.

"Look," Melissa said, "I'm not wild about going out in the woods and watching a bunch of dogs chase a helpless raccoon, but I've got to, and I've got to do this on my own. Jim's father's resisting the idea of his son having to come here after school, and I'm afraid if either Gwenn or I don't convince the man that what we're doing is for Jim's good, he might pull the boy out of the program."

"So?" asked Derek.

"So Jim is exactly the type of child we want to help. He's bright. He has a lot of potential. And unless something is done, he'll drop out of school the moment he turns sixteen."

"I still don't see what this has to do with my going tonight."

She tapped a finger against his chest. "He asked me, not you."

"And I'm inviting myself along." He looked down at her hand, and Melissa pulled back.

Touching him was not a wise idea. There was too much raw power in the man, too much magnetism. Nevertheless, she tried to stand firm. "And what if I say you can't go?"

He smiled and chucked her under her chin. "I'm going."

End of argument, she realized. Ranting and raving on her part wouldn't accomplish a thing. But giving in to Derek didn't mean she'd let him take control. "In that case, you're to stay in the background. This is my chance to get to know Jim's father, find out what I can about the man."

"Fine. That's what I want, too."

"No threatening him."

"I wouldn't think of it."

"No attacking every bush looking for bogeymen."

"Only if they're there."

"You're simply coming along as a friend." She'd have to give Jim and his father some reason why Derek was joining them. "You've never been on a coon hunt and were interested, so I invited you along."

"Sounds good to me." He quirked an eyebrow. "Have you ever been on a coon hunt?"

"Never."

"So what do we do?"

Melissa laughed lightly. "I guess that's what we find out tonight."

The moon was just coming up when Jim's father parked his battered old pickup in front of the house. Melissa had been watching for it and saw Jim jump out. She had the door open before he reached the porch. From an aluminum box on the bed of the truck came the constant barking of dogs, their mournful bays announcing to all that they knew where they were going and were eager to get there.

Jim stopped in front of her, his gaze skipping from her long-sleeved paisley print blouse to her jeans to the boots he'd said she should wear. Melissa hoped she was dressed appropriately. With such short notice, it was the best she could do.

"Is this okay?" she asked, stepping back to grab the denim jacket she'd left by the door.

The boy didn't answer. His gaze had moved higher.

Derek was coming down the stairs. He was also wearing boots and his new jeans and one of the flannel shirts he'd bought. His jacket was slung over his arm. He glanced at the boy, then looked outside at the truck. "We can't all fit in that," he said. "Jim, tell your father Miss Davenport and I will follow him in my car."

"Yore goin', too?" The boy's eyes widened, then narrowed.

"Mr. Vincetti has never been on a coon hunt and thought it sounded interesting."

For a second Jim didn't move, simply stared at Derek, then he turned and ran back to the truck.

"First hurdle over." Derek pulled the door closed behind them and gently pressed his hand against the small of Melissa's back, guiding her toward his rental car. He hoped the rest of the evening would go as smoothly. After making a fool of himself that afternoon, he didn't need any more situations where he'd have to justify his actions.

He was helping Missy into the car when he looked up and noticed Jim's father had gotten out of the truck. The man was tall and thin, his sharp features and a stubble of beard accentuated by the streetlight. Derek smiled and waved. It seemed the friendly thing to do, and he'd promised Melissa he'd be friendly. The man simply stared, then turned away, got back into his truck and slammed the door shut.

Derek tried not to let the man's actions bother him, but they did. Not on a personal level, but deeper, where his basic intuition resided. Something was wrong.

Or maybe he was getting paranoid. As he followed the pickup out of town and into the mountains, he wondered if Missy was right, if he was letting his job turn him into a suspicious cynic.

One more reason to consider a change.

Of course, being prepared for the unexpected wasn't a bad idea. The moon was in its last quarter and the night was dark. "You did bring those flashlights, didn't you?" Derek asked.

"I told you I would. One for me, one for you." She pulled one from her jacket pocket and set it on the dash.

"And the compass?"

"Oh, darn!" That she'd forgotten. "Do you really think we'll need one?"

He hoped not.

"I mean," she went on, "I don't plan on going off on my own, and Jim's dad should have a compass, shouldn't he?"

"I imagine he will," Derek agreed. If he'd known he'd be hiking in the woods, he would have bought a compass and flashlight that afternoon.

"You know, I'm really kind of looking forward to this. Not the hunt, but going into the woods at night. It should be beautiful." Melissa twisted in her seat and gazed out the side window.

The movement stirred the scent of her perfume, and Derek breathed deeply. She never put on so much that it was overpowering, just enough to tease and distract. If the situation were different, he'd also be looking forward to this evening. Not to being in the woods, but being with her.

Only the situation wasn't different. His job was to keep track of a headstrong heiress. Which meant, cynical or not, he'd be keeping a close eye on Jim's father.

The dogs—three rangy, tricolored Tennessee Walkers—barked and strained at the ends of their ropes. Hank Allerton tied them to the pickup's bumper, then pulled a light attached to a twelve-volt battery out of his truck and strapped the battery pack around his waist. When he switched on the light, a large circle illuminated the woods in front of them. Allerton twisted the lens, focusing the light down to a smaller, more intense beam, then aimed it at the tops of the tress.

Pines and cedars, as tall as multistoried buildings covered the steep slope of the mountain. There wasn't a house in sight, and no cars on the road. The baying of the hounds covered most sounds, but during a moment of quiet, Melissa heard the hoot of an owl somewhere off in the distance. It could have come straight out of a horror movie, and she shivered and slipped on her jacket, patting the flashlight she still had in her pocket. Maybe a walk in the woods wasn't such a good idea. Once they were under those trees, not much moonlight would be filtering through.

She'd never been afraid of the dark, but an uneasy chill skittered down her spine. Maybe it was because she didn't know the area. Or maybe it was the way Jim's father kept looking at her, never directly and honestly, but always out of the corner of his eye. She hated to admit it, but the man gave her the creeps.

Derek also slipped on his jacket then began using some of the insect repellant Hank Allerton had given him. The coon hunter had warned them that even though the cool nights were cutting down on the mosquito population, ticks still presented a problem. Derek liberally covered his jeans and exposed skin.

Melissa was more concerned with larger animals. "You ever run into any bears when you're coon hunting, Mr. Allerton?"

"Not too often."

She watched him reach into his truck. His answer hadn't reassured her.

"Let me get your legs," Derek said and kneeled in front of her.

He began rubbing his hands over her pant legs, the motion of his strokes sure and quick as he spread the protective repellant across her jeans. Then his fingers moved to the insides of her thighs, and his strokes slowed.

Melissa tensed, the heat radiating from his hands stoking an internal fire she couldn't stop. Maybe in her mind she'd vowed to treat him coolly, let him know he couldn't betray her and have her fawning all over him, but her body wasn't responding that way. Placing a hand on his shoulder, she reached down for the bottle. "Thanks, but I can finish."

"Just make sure you're protected. Ticks spread diseases, and I don't want to take you back sick."

Take her back. Derek's only concern was for her safety. He wanted to deliver her hale and hearty to her father. She should have known better than to let his touch get her hot and bothered.

"Y'all ever tried any moonshine?" Hank Allerton asked, coming up beside Derek.

"No." Derek stood slowly, eyeing the mason jar in the man's hand. The liquid it held was perfectly clear.

"Try some." Allerton unscrewed the lid and held the jar toward Derek.

Derek knew what he'd just done with Melissa, rubbing her legs and getting himself aroused, had been stupid. He wasn't about to add to that stupidity by taking a drink. Without hesitation, he shook his head. "No, thanks, I don't drink."

"Come on now. Ya don't want me thinkin' yore too good to drink with a mountain man, do ya?"

Melissa recognized the challenge. It was in the look Allerton gave Derek, in the man's tone and his stance. She also knew she didn't want Derek accepting it. Reaching out, she took the jar Allerton held. "I'd love to try some. I've heard so much about this stuff."

"Don't—" Allerton tried to warn, but she took a large swallow before he finished.

White Lightning. She suddenly knew how the name had come about. She felt as though she'd been struck by lightning. Gasoline couldn't have burned more. She'd drunk martinis and Tequila sunrises, which were supposed to pack a kick, but this wasn't a kick, it was a punch in the chest. Gagging and coughing, Melissa nearly doubled over.

Allerton grabbed the jar, and Derek grabbed her, holding her close. She clung to his arm and gasped for a breath. Never had air seemed so precious or a person to lean on so welcome. Slowly the burning subsided and air filled her lungs.

"Good stuff," she rasped, and Jim started laughing.

"Sure can tell yore an outsider," the boy said.

"You should just sip it if yore not used to it," advised Allerton. Again he held the jar toward Derek. "Come on, try some."

It was almost an order, and Melissa felt Derek tense. Before he could answer, she again reached for the jar. "Believe me, Mr. Allerton, you don't want him drinking. When he drinks, he gets meaner than a razorback hog. But I'd like to try it again."

This time Melissa took a small sip of the liquid. Derek, Allerton and Jim watched her closely. She smiled and tried to act as though she were used to drinking one-hundred-plus proof corn whiskey. Smacking her lips, she handed the jar back to Jim's father. "You make this yourself?"

"Friend did."

Jim supplied the name. "Orrie Andrews. Him and his brother Billy Joe are always bringin' some to the house. They was talkin' about you today, Miz Davenport. They said—"

"Get the dogs, boy," Allerton abruptly ordered, cutting the boy off. "Now!"

Jim turned away and headed for the pickup's tailgate. "I'll help him," Derek offered, and followed.

The dogs were lunging about and barking, but Derek tried to keep his voice low when he spoke to Jim. "What did your father's friends say about Miss Davenport?"

Jim glanced at his father. The man was watching them. Glaring. Quickly the boy began untying the dogs. "Nut'in'."

"But you were about to tell us something."

Again Jim glanced at his father. "Just that it were funny she'd come here to work." The third dog freed, the boy faced Derek. "Ya know what I mean? Her havin' so much money and all. Did her pa really pay to git her back?"

"Jim Bob, git over here," Allerton yelled.

The boy didn't wait for Derek's answer. Quick as a rabbit, he hurried to his father's side, leaving Derek by the truck wondering just what Allerton and his friends had discussed.

Within minutes the three hounds disappeared into the woods, baying as they ran. Allerton and Jim didn't move, just listened until the dogs had traveled some distance. Then Allerton glanced at his watch. "We'd better git."

Derek stepped to Melissa's side, but Hank Allerton shook his head. "Me and Miz Davenport got some talkin' to do 'bout the boy. You and Jim Bob go on ahead. We'll catch up when the dogs go ta tree."

Derek didn't move. No way was he leaving Missy alone with Allerton. "I'll stay back with Miss Davenport."

His tone was firm and decisive. Beyond question. Allerton momentarily looked perplexed, then shrugged and changed his order. "Jim Bob, go on and catch up with them dogs. I'll stay back with your teacher and her boyfriend."

"Derek's not—"

Derek cut her off, his arm going around her shoulders. "Now, now, Missy. I think Mr. Allerton knows what's up."

Hank Allerton would probably think the look in Derek's eyes was love. Melissa knew better. Although Derek smiled and even brushed a light kiss across her forehead, his gaze held a message of warning. He was worrying about her safety again. Overreacting to a simple suggestion that they split up. Being paranoid.

"You'll have to excuse us, Mr. Allerton," she said, grinning. She'd play along. In fact, she'd more than play along. "Derek and I haven't seen each other for a long time." Wrapping an arm around Derek's waist, she snuggled closer. "Have we, honey?"

"No, we haven't." He cocked his eyebrows, and she knew he wondered what she'd do next.

A hiccup took her by surprise, shaking her body. She giggled, then quickly took in a deep breath. She wasn't the giggling type, but suddenly everything seemed very funny. Derek pretending to be her boyfriend. Allerton's frown. Jim turning his back on them.

Again she hiccupped.

"Sorry," she apologized, trying to suppress a laugh.

Hank Allerton snorted. "You drink any more of this stuff, and you'll be crocked." He took another swallow of the moonshine, then looked at his watch. Quickly he wiped his lips on his sleeve. "Jim Bob, you git on now." Allerton faced Derek and Melissa. "You two follow me."

The man's concern about the time bothered Derek. Why would a raccoon or a dog care what time it was? They'd follow, but not too closely, and he wasn't letting Melissa out of his sight.

Going through the woods, it was impossible to walk side by side, but Derek kept contact with Melissa, sometimes holding on to the back of her jacket, sometimes resting his hand on her shoulder. Even after five minutes she still had the hiccups, her body jerking with each attack. She'd hold her breath, then gasp for air, only to have another hit.

A loud one caused Allerton to turn around and look back. "Sorry," she again apologized.

Allerton grunted and once again checked his watch. "Come on," he ordered and pushed on.

Another hiccup racked Melissa's body, and Derek gave her shoulder a squeeze. Sometimes his mother would get the hiccups when she drank. She'd tell him to scare her. So he'd try.

When she was drunk, she always scared him.

Thinking of a way to scare Melissa while walking through the woods was a challenge. He could pretend he was a bear. Or...

Derek pulled Melissa to a stop, turned her and kissed her. He did it so quickly that she didn't have a chance to say anything. That was the idea—to surprise her. Shock her. Take her breath away.

And he could feel her surprise, hear her quick intake of breath. But then she began to react. Her hands went to his shoulders and her mouth moved against his. And he was the one who was surprised. Not by what she was doing, but by his reaction.

Where was his control? Why did he want to claim this woman as his? Never let her go?

Immediately he pulled away. "I—I was trying..." he stammered.

She giggled.

"I was trying to scare you."

"Your kisses don't scare me."

So he'd discovered.

"You two comin'?" Allerton yelled back at them.

Once again Melissa giggled. "He's sure in a hurry."

"Too much so."

"We're coming, Mr. Allerton," she called and followed the coon hunter, stepping over fallen branches and around briars that caught on her clothing. If she hoped to make a good impression on Jim's father, she needed to get hold of herself, stop giggling and forget Derek. As if that were possible with the man directly behind her.

"You're not going to kill any raccoons tonight, are you?" she called after him. "Jim said this was just a training run."

"Can't kill 'em. Season ain't open yet."

That was a relief. "Jim said you had a new dog."

"Yup."

"Actually he said you've got the best dogs around," she went on, hoping to get the man talking.

"Yup."

He wasn't helping, but she kept trying. "How can you tell which way to go?"

"I kin tell."

Long-distance yelling wasn't creating the rapport she'd hoped to achieve. Increasing her pace, she caught up with Jim's father, Derek staying close behind. "You have a nice boy," she said, no longer having to yell. "He's really quite smart. We hope—"

Allerton interrupted her with a snort. "It's a waste of his time, his goin' ta yore house. This after-school stuff ain't gettin' ma wood split."

"I'm sure what we're doing seems like a waste of your son's time, but . . ."

Derek listened as Melissa tried to convince the man that Jim's going to the Learning House would benefit both of them. She had some good arguments, he thought, though most of the time Allerton merely snorted or grunted, pausing occasionally for another swig from the jar of moonshine.

One thing Derek noticed—his kiss had worked. Melissa's hiccups were gone. Another thing he realized was that they were moving down the mountain slope—practically the opposite direction from where the dogs were barking. Finally he spoke up. "Mr. Allerton, aren't your dogs behind us and to the left?"

The coon hunter stopped, snapped on his light and shined it directly in Derek's face. "Mister, you ever been huntin' in these here mountains?"

Derek squinted and used a hand to shield his eyes from the bright light. "No."

"You wasn't born here, didn't grow up 'round these parts, so you don't know about the vibrations, do ya?"

Derek was picking up vibrations. Hostile ones. "No, I don't."

Allerton snapped off his light and took a long swig from the bottle before he spoke again. "These here hawlers makes everythin' sound different. Vibrates the barkin'. Shore, ma two old hounds is behind us, but that new one, the one I wants to see run, he's straight ahead. Course, if ya wants to go off on yer own . . ." He paused and chuckled. "Just don't go steppin' on any snakes or disturbin' any bars."

Melissa cringed at that idea. "Don't you worry about Jim being off on his own?"

"Jim Bob's use ta bein' on his own."

Derek had a feeling he and Missy needed to be on their own, too. He didn't want Melissa thinking him crazy, but he wasn't buying Allerton's story about the hollows vibrating the sound. He'd also swear there wasn't any dog straight ahead of them, new or old. What he had heard—below them and only seconds before—was a car... or a truck. Whichever, it needed a new muffler. And it had stopped.

"How far are we from a road?" he asked.

"A ways. No more questions now. I wanna listen to ma dog. Nut'in' prettier than the sound of a hound hot on a track." Allerton turned his back to them and started down the slope.

Derek continued listening. He'd still swear all three hounds were behind them, but then he did hear a dog bark below them. The bay of the hound was long and woeful.

A new sound.

Allerton picked up his pace, but Derek caught Melissa and stopped her. With a finger to his lips, he signalled for her to say nothing then took her hand and started toward the left.

"Derek, what are you doing?" she asked, resisting.

"Shh," he warned. Allerton was quite a way ahead of them, but the man could have heard her. "Follow me."

She looked after Allerton, then in the direction Derek was facing. "We can't just take off."

"Missy, you've known me for eight years. You've known him an hour. Do this for me, please."

It wasn't fair. He was asking her to make a decision with her heart not her head. "What about the snakes and bears?"

Derek was pretty sure the only snakes they needed to worry about were ahead of them. "We'll be careful."

"But why?"

Derek knew he couldn't explain why he felt it imperative to get her away from Allerton. One couldn't explain the smell of danger. Or the sense of it. But having that ability had kept him alive more than once during his lifetime. "Just trust me."

She really had no choice. She squeezed his hand and followed.

Chapter Eight

Derek kept his light pointed low and straight ahead, and Melissa stayed close behind him. They headed back up the mountainside, moving quickly and quietly through the trees, angling toward the long, woeful, baying of the coon hounds.

Below them a single dog barked, and within minutes Allerton called their names. His yells at first sounded concerned, then took on a note of desperation. Derek stopped to listen, and Melissa halted beside him.

"This is ridiculous," she whispered. "A teacher doesn't run off and hide from a student's father."

"I know you think I'm paranoid, but something was wrong," Derek insisted, his voice hushed.

"You mean about the dogs? He explained that."

"He gave us some bull about vibrations. Come on, Missy, you didn't really believe that, did you? And there was no dog ahead of us, not until that car—or truck—stopped."

She hated to admit it, but she hadn't heard a dog ahead of them, either, not until after Derek questioned Allerton about the direction they were headed. And the vibrations theory had sounded strange. "Okay, so he's a little confused about what he's hearing. The man's drunk."

"And worried about the time. Ever since he got out of his truck, he's been checking his watch, like he has to be somewhere at a certain time."

"Maybe..." She couldn't think of a reason to explain Allerton's concern with the time or his push to keep moving.

Derek had his own ideas. "Maybe we'd better see if we can find those other dogs and Jim Bob."

Allerton kept calling, but they moved on.

Step after step, she followed Derek. Time became an irrelevant concept, distances more important. There was the distance they'd covered and how far they had to go, the only known fact being the sound of the hounds. Sometimes the mournful baying disappeared entirely, blocked by earth, rocks and trees as their steps took them into a hollow. It was then that Melissa worried that they'd never hear the dogs again, that they'd never find their way out of the woods. Yet she'd put her faith in Derek when he first asked her to follow him, and she still trusted him to get them to safety.

Her trust was verified when they came out of the next hollow. There was no doubt the dogs were straight ahead. She wanted to move quickly, get to the hounds before there was a chance they'd stop barking. Derek, however, slowed his steps, approaching the area quietly and cautiously.

If he expected an ambush or a trap of some kind, he didn't find one. All Melissa saw were three tricolored hounds circling and barking up a large oak tree, and Jim stretched out on a log, gazing at the stars above. The boy started when she called his name, immediately sitting up, then scrambling to his feet. The Walkers continued chopping off barks, always looking up into the leafy branches, only occasionally taking time to pant and circle to a new location.

"Took you guys long enough," Jim complained, brushing bits of bark from his ragged jeans and looking beyond them. "Where's Pa?"

"We got separated from him," lied Derek.

Jim slouched sullenly. "You mean we gotta wait for him now?"

"Actually, Missy... Miss Davenport and I need to be getting back. Any way you can get those dogs to leave that tree so you can take us to the car?"

"Pull 'em?" Jim looked at the dogs.

One of the coon hounds had stopped barking and was gazing their way, his tongue lolling out the side of his mouth and his panting audible. The other two kept on barking.

"S'ppose I could," the boy decided then calculatingly smiled at Derek. "How much is it worth to ya?"

Intimidation was one of Derek's fortes. It wasn't what he said as much as the way he said it, the way he presented the message. Two steps took him close to the boy—threateningly close—then Derek dropped his voice to a low, lethal pitch. "Pull them."

Jim tried staring him down, but he'd lost before he even began, and soon Jim was yelling at the dogs, going to them, praising them, grabbing collars and snapping on ropes. "Bully," Melissa muttered just loud enough for Derek to hear.

"Now, you wouldn't want me giving him money, would you?" He kept an eye on Jim, but Derek's posture was relaxed. "Next thing you know, the kid would be hustling little old ladies and fleecing unsuspecting tourists."

"All because of you." Melissa hated to think it, but Jim was probably already hustling little old ladies and fleecing tourists.

"I think I'll give him a hand," Derek said. Jim was a good-sized kid and strong, but the three dogs weren't ready to leave, not without seeing the raccoon they were sure was up that tree. One had already wrapped its rope around Jim's legs, and the other was circling the boy the opposite direction. The third refused to be caught.

"That's the new one," Jim explained, his frustration evident.

"Let me help you," Derek said.

The boy didn't object and handed over both ropes and went after the third dog.

Derek was surprised by the pull the two dogs exerted. The hounds weren't much more than two feet in height at the shoulders and lean to the point where their ribs showed, but the animals had only one idea—to get to the raccoon up that tree.

Even after Jim caught the third hound, and Derek jerked and dragged the two Walkers he held away from the tree, the dogs continued barking. It was some time and some distance before they quit, the sound replaced by loud panting and every so often a plaintive whine. Walking through the woods became a challenge, even after the hounds stopped pulling. Every scent crossed had to be sniffed, every bush marked.

They'd traveled quite a way before Derek glanced back at Melissa. "You okay?"

"Sure. Couldn't be better." She scoffed. "Coon hunting is definitely something I don't like. And I can think of a lot better ways to spend a Saturday night than hiking up and down mountainsides."

"It was your idea to come."

"It wasn't my idea to take off on our own."

"You left Pa?" Jim questioned, picking up on what she'd said.

"Got separated from him," Derek quickly corrected. "Your father drink a lot?"

Jim didn't answer.

"My father used to drink a lot," Derek went on. "So did my mother."

"My ma died when I were a baby," Jim said. "Fever got her."

"The drinking got my mother. I was ten when she died. Seventeen when my father died."

"Sometimes I wish my pa were dead," Jim confessed, then quickly looked away and yelled at the dog he had and jerked on its rope.

Derek knew the boy was afraid of what he'd just said. "That's a natural feeling. I used to feel that way, too. Especially whenever my father beat me."

"Your pa beat you, too?" Jim glanced back, his expression less antagonistic.

"He'd be drinking, and I'd say something that would cross him, and he'd hit me. Then the next day, when he'd sobered up, he'd tell me he was sorry and that he'd never do it again. He'd promise to do all sorts of things, but of course that's all they were—promises. Nothing ever changed. It got so that after a while I didn't trust him, didn't trust anyone. I was really confused back then. I felt guilty because my mother had died and felt somehow it was my fault, but then Dad would start hitting me, and I'd wish he were dead."

Melissa saw Jim nod and knew Derek was touching feelings the boy shared. It was the most she'd ever heard Derek talk about his family and his childhood. Although he didn't hesitate to say his parents had been alcoholics and his brother was one, that was about as much as he ever went into the matter.

Derek kept talking to Jim. "You know, kids who live with alcoholics need someone to talk to, someone they can trust. I was lucky. A policeman took me under his wing. He gave me a place where I could go whenever my father got mean. Sergeant Hull's home became like a safe house for me. The Learning House would be a good place for someone who needed help to go. Gwenn—Mrs. Bradley—is someone a person could turn to if things got rough."

"What could she do?" Jim asked, his tone just a little surly.

"She's a good listener, and sometimes it just helps to talk about what's going on instead of keeping it all inside."

"And we always have a couch you could sleep on," said Melissa, picking up on the message Derek was trying to get across.

Jim looked at her. "Orrie Andrews said maybe my bein' made to go to your house after school weren't so bad after all, that somethin' good might come of it. Maybe he's right."

Derek knew then that he needed to find out more about Orrie Andrews.

Melissa was glad the boy knew the way back to the truck and car. She didn't have the slightest idea where they were and was completely surprised when they came out onto the dirt road and saw Jim's father's old truck and Derek's rental car only a hundred yards away. What she didn't see was Jim's father, and her guilt over leaving the man returned. "Now what do we do?" she asked Derek

"Go get in the car," he ordered. "As soon as I help Jim put up these dogs, we're leaving."

"I'm not going to go off and leave him." Not with his father possibly passed out somewhere back in the woods.

"Then we'll take him wi—"

The sound of a vehicle coming up the road, its muffler giving off a loud roar as the driver accelerated, stopped Derek. The roar grew louder, increasingly closer. Suddenly a truck came careering around the corner, its headlights slashing across tree trunks, then zeroing in on them.

Blinded by the brightness, Melissa shielded her eyes. She didn't think to move. It was Derek who jerked her and the two dogs he held over to the side. Protectively he stepped in front of her.

With a squeal of brakes, bald tires skidded on loose gravel, and the truck came to an abrupt stop. A dog in a box on the bed of the truck barked, starting the ones Derek and Jim held to join in. The driver didn't dim or turn off his lights, and Derek was harshly silhouetted in front of her.

Over the barking, he called back at her. "Be ready to run!"

She was set to go, his tension catching.

Slowly the door on the passenger's side opened. The barking dogs made hearing almost impossible, and she could barely see past the glare of the headlights, but when she edged to Derek's side, she could tell it was a man getting out of the truck... and it looked like Allerton.

As soon as he was out, he slammed the door. With a grinding of gears, the driver of the truck put it into reverse, backed up a few feet, then made a sharp U-turn. Once the headlights moved off them, she could see there were two men inside—the driver and a passenger. She also saw it was a green truck. A dusty, dented, drab green.

"You dawgs, shaddup!" Hank Allerton yelled, his voice barely carrying over the baying of the hounds and the roar of the truck as it vanished down the road.

Staggering slightly, he walked toward Derek. In his left hand he held a mason jar, this one nearly full. "Shaddup, you mangy critters!" he yelled again.

To her surprise, the dogs stopped barking, the two Derek held slinking to the ground and warily watching the man as he neared.

"Where the hell did you two git off to?" Allerton demanded.

"We got lost," she and Derek said, almost in unison, immediately they glanced at each other.

"Lost?" The moonshine had thickened his drawl and the word sounded foreign.

"I had to find the little girls' room," Melissa said.

"I had to relieve myself," Derek answered at the same time.

Again they glanced at each other, then grinned.

"I yelled for ya." Allerton was watching both of them. He was also swaying on his feet, and considering how much moonshine she'd seen him consume, Melissa didn't really see how the man was still standing.

"Must be those vibrations you were telling us about," Derek said, absolutely stone-faced. "We heard you yelling, but we thought you'd gotten up above us. It was purely by luck that we came across your boy and the dogs. He's the one who showed us the way back here."

"Some luck." Allerton eyed Derek suspiciously, then looked at his son.

"I didn't want to leave the tree, Pa," Jim said quickly. "He made me."

Allerton didn't respond, just opened the jar he held and took a swig. He stared at Derek the entire time he was drinking, even when he smacked his lips, then wiped them with his sleeve.

Derek never looked away. "How'd you ever manage to find a ride?" he asked.

"Purely by luck," Allerton answered.

Stalemate, Melissa decided. Neither man was going to tell the truth, the entire evening had turned into a fiasco and she was tired. "As long as we're all back, I'd like to get home."

"I'll put these dogs up," Derek said. "You go get into the car."

Hank Allerton glanced down at the two dogs Derek held, then at the one wrapping itself around Jim's legs. That they'd found all three with Jim was obvious. "See ya got the new one," he said. "Musta doubled back ta them others."

Derek didn't think so, but he didn't argue.

Jim already had the dog box open, and the dog he'd been leading jumped in. Willingly the two hounds

Derek held also jumped onto the bed of the truck, then went into the aluminum box. As he undid their ropes, he spoke to Jim, keeping his voice low. "I think your father's had too much to drink. Why don't you ride back with us?"

The boy looked at his father, then down at the ground. He said nothing, just kicked the dirt by the tailgate with the toe of his boot, then shook his head.

He couldn't force Jim to go with them, though he wished he could. "Don't forget what I said, if you ever need help, the Learning House is a place you can go," Derek reminded him.

Jim continued kicking dirt. He didn't answer, and Derek didn't push. The boy had heard.

Under other circumstances, he would have stayed to make sure Allerton didn't harm the boy—at least not in his presence—but at the moment, getting Melissa out of these hills was more urgent. The two in the green pickup had left, but there was no telling how far they'd gone, or if they might be back.

He hurried to the car.

"I'd hoped this evening would improve my relationship with Jim and his father," Melissa said after Derek got in. "Now he'll probably pull Jim out of the program. We shouldn't have taken off."

"What should we have done—let those two guys in the green pickup give us a ride? Or more specifically, you a ride?" He scoffed and started the engine. "They would have liked that. It's what they had planned."

"You're crazy!" she exclaimed.

"Am I? From the moment we left this spot, Allerton knew exactly where he was going and what time he had to be there. He didn't expect me to be along, but since I was, he tried to get me drunk. He probably planned on leaving me, passed out, somewhere in the woods. Only you spoiled that idea."

"Jim's father was just being friendly when he offered you some moonshine," she insisted.

"Was he being friendly when he tried to send me off with Jim, leaving you with him?"

"He wanted to talk."

"He wanted you by yourself so they could kidnap you."

Melissa shook her head. "You're paranoid, Derek. Absolutely paranoid."

Maybe he was. After all, the men in the green truck had simply turned around and driven off. Nevertheless, Derek drove back to Red Oak with as much speed as was safe on the twisting, narrow road, and he kept close watch for anything unusual.

Melissa said nothing, and the warmth they'd shared on the drive earlier was gone. He missed it more than he wanted to admit, but he didn't know what else to say. He was sure something had been wrong tonight. Felt it in his gut.

He gave a relieved sigh when he parked the car in front of the Learning House. Maybe it wasn't a fortress, but he felt safer here than in the woods. Switching off the engine, he turned toward her. "I can't prove it, but you are in danger, Missy. I'm sure of that."

"It's Melissa, not Missy. Remember?" she corrected, and unsnapped her seat belt. "And I wouldn't be in danger if you hadn't told Mary Sue my life story."

He touched her arm before she opened the door. "No matter what you think I did not tell that newspaper woman a thing about you. At least not directly."

Pausing, she looked at him. "Derek, don't lie to me."

"I'm not." He pulled his hand back, released his own seat belt and tried to explain. "Look, I'm sorry. You're right, it was my fault that story was printed. But I didn't talk to that woman. She was behind me when I was on the phone to your father. I should have known she was there, but I didn't."

He scoffed at his own ineptitude. "I'm not the security man I'd like people to think I am."

"So Derek Vincetti made a mistake." Melissa rather liked the idea.

For some reason she couldn't stay angry with this man, not for long. Instead of getting out, she turned in her seat to face him. "And here I thought you were perfect."

"Hardly."

"That makes two."

"Two what?"

"Two mistakes I know you've made. This one and when you married Carolyn."

"Let's hope this mistake isn't that disastrous."

She wanted to reach out and touch him, but she held back. "Do you still love her?"

"No." He gave a dry laugh. "Now that I look back, I wonder why I ever married her. Stupidity, I guess. At least that's what you told me, as I recall."

Melissa remembered. Painfully remembered. "That day you called and said you were getting married, you told me she was the most beautiful woman in the world."

"That was before I'd seen her drink a fifth of gin. She could be ugly then. Very ugly."

"Didn't you know she drank before you married her?" It had seemed ironic that the child of alcoholic parents would marry an alcoholic.

"I knew she drank. I didn't know how much she drank. I guess you did. You tried to warn me."

"Actually I never knew Carolyn that well. She'd graduated before I started high school, but I often saw her at the country club with her parents. And I'd heard stories about her. I'm afraid I never liked her. She used people."

Derek gave a snort. "Funny. That's exactly what she said I did. Used people."

"Well, she was wrong."

"And how do you know?" There was a defensive cynicism to his tone.

"Because I've heard stories about you, too. A user doesn't take time to find a house for a homeless family, coach boys' summer league baseball and try to get his wife to attend AA meetings."

"She said I did that to make her look bad. Look, Missy, don't go making me into a saint. Maybe she's right. Back when I met Carolyn, I was trying my darnedest to move up in society. Maybe I did use her."

"You mean you decided to marry rich and went after her?"

"No." He chuckled. "She was the one who did the 'going after.' We met at a dinner party your father had asked me to attend, and from that night on, Carolyn called me day and night. I was flattered. Actually—" he chuckled again, remembering "—I couldn't believe it. There she was, beautiful, well educated and rich, and she was throwing herself at me, a guy from the wrong part of town. Nevertheless, looking back, I'm not sure if I was just blinded by what was happening or if down deep I didn't decide to take advantage of it."

She'd bet on blinded.

"One thing being married to Carolyn taught me is that buying tailor-made clothes, driving an expensive car, going to all the right parties and mingling with all the right people doesn't mean you'll be accepted by the rich." He looked directly at her. "I'm through trying to be what I'm not, and I won't be blinded a second time."

"Don't go judging me by Carolyn."

How should he judge her? She was beautiful. Maybe not gorgeous, but cute and pretty. And she was certainly well educated and rich. That she aroused in him desires he shouldn't have, couldn't have, frightened him. "You should marry Paul."

"Why, so he can merge his father's company with my father's?"

"Because he's the right kind of man for you. From what I heard, you two were quite a hot item last spring."

"Where'd you hear that?"

"At work." He again touched the sleeve of her jacket. "Next time you use your father's office for a rendezvous, you should lock the door."

"I don't use my father's office for rendezvous." But she knew what he was talking about. "Paul was meeting me at the plant that day, and we were going out to lunch. We were in Daddy's office, and Paul kissed me and—"

Melissa paused, remembering the incident in detail. Paul's kiss had taken her by surprise, especially when his hand slipped under her blouse. It had been that day—that moment—she realized she didn't love him. It had also been that moment her father's secretary opened the door.

"He kissed me, and we went to lunch," she finished. "I like Paul, but that's all."

"He's got everything a woman like you should want. Looks. Money. A secure future."

"Maybe I don't want all those things." *Maybe I just want you.* How she wished she could make him see that. "Derek, the kind of security I need is emotional. Paul couldn't give me that. As I've said, he's a nice guy, but..."

"But," he repeated with just a hint of a chuckle.

"I kinda like guys who sneak in back doors to rescue damsels from terrorists who don't exist."

He cleared his throat and pulled his hand back. "I have a feeling you're not going to let me forget that one."

"Nope." She missed the feel of his touch, and knew he was purposefully trying to distance himself. She didn't intend to let him.

Reaching over, she ran her fingers spiderlike up his jacket sleeve, the feel of the fabric smooth, of the man hard. "I think you owe me," she said, her tone as sultry as the air in the car.

Her fingertips traveled to the side of his neck, and she felt the heat of his body and the throb of his pulse.

"How's that?" he rasped, then quickly cleared his throat.

"Grabbing me the way you did." Her thumb grazed his chin, a hint of stubble rough against her skin. She heard him suck in a breath, the sound as ragged as a dying man's last gasp. "Scaring me."

The dim light filtering in from the streetlight outside softened his Roman features. She traced the curve of his cheek, then let her hand roam to the back of his neck. Weaving her fingers into thick, virile hair, she whispered, "Kiss me, Derek."

"You don't know what you're asking," he groaned.

Oh, but she did. She wanted him to stop being Derek Vincetti the protector, her father's errand boy. She wanted him to react like a man...like a lover. "Kiss me," she repeated, and pressed her fingertips against the back of his head, leaning forward as she drew his face toward hers.

He was strength and compassion, and she needed him, just as he needed her. Melissa knew that as clearly as she knew her name. Closing her eyes, she parted her lips.

She could feel his breath, his warmth and his longing. He might say they didn't belong together, but he didn't believe it, not really. She would make him forget the past; this was right.

Then suddenly, a hairsbreadth away, he pulled back, separating himself from her hold. "No," he said harshly, the single word a slap to the face.

"Derek," she pleaded, staring at him, stunned, and shaking with her own need.

"It's time to go in, Missy."

His tone was controlled and withdrawn. Stiffening, she raised her own defenses. "When are you going to stop thinking of me as a child? The name is Melissa, not Missy."

She regally got out of the car and walked to the house.

Chapter Nine

"So how did the coon hunt go?" Gwenn asked the next morning.

Melissa turned from getting two coffee mugs out of the cupboard and looked toward the kitchen table.

Derek held his head up with his hands, his eyes still blurry. Melissa wasn't surprised he looked tired. After he'd refused to kiss her, they'd gone inside and directly to their rooms, but for a long time she'd heard him toss and turn in his bed. How long he'd stayed awake, she didn't know. Emotional and physical exhaustion finally vanquished her confused thoughts, and she slept soundly until the sun brightened her room and the lisping, dreamy song of a warbler woke her.

It was after she'd done her exercises, taken a shower and started the coffee that Derek had come downstairs. Their conversation was stilted, neither mentioning the night before. Now she waited for him to answer Gwenn.

"The coon hunt was interesting," he said.

An understatement if Melissa had ever heard one.

Gwenn also got herself a mug. "Did you see any raccoons?"

Melissa answered. "No, but the dogs insisted there was one up a tree." She brought two mugs of coffee to the table, setting one in front of Derek. "My bodyguard, here, also insists there were some snakes in the grass last night."

"I always worry about snakes," said Gwenn, opening the refrigerator door and studying its contents.

"These were the two-legged type he was worried about," Melissa explained.

Gwenn's head popped up, her eyebrows raised, and Derek took over. "Our host was acting a little strange and led us away from the dogs, not to them. He also 'just happened' to run into some men who gave him a ride back to the truck."

"Our host was drunk, and he ran into a couple of other coon hunters. That's all," Melissa argued.

"I'm afraid Jim's father is drunk a good deal of the time. What would you like for breakfast, Derek? Some good old-fashioned Southern grits?"

Melissa grinned when he looked at her for an answer. "Try them. And just in case you're not wild about grits, how do a couple of eggs and sausages sound?"

"Sounds high in cholesterol and great."

The kitchen took on a warm, homey atmosphere, Gwenn preparing the grits and toast, Melissa frying eggs and sausage patties. Derek relaxed in his chair and enjoyed the moment. Living alone, he often skipped breakfast or ate out. And even when he'd been married, if he'd wanted anything for breakfast, he was usually the one to prepare it. For Carolyn, a hangover and eggs didn't go together.

He also enjoyed watching Melissa move around the kitchen, her orange-and-pink sweatshirt as bright as the sun rays coming through the windows and her faded jeans emphasizing every curve and dimple in her slender hips and thighs. Her hair had a fresh-washed look and curled in a tangle that framed her face. If she'd slept as poorly as he had, it certainly didn't show.

He felt whipped. Physically he wasn't used to hiking up and down steep slopes. Emotionally he was finding it very difficult to think of Missy as the boss's daughter and not a delectable, determined and desirable lady. What he needed was to get her back to California and her father. Then maybe he'd start sleeping better. "Gwenn, do you know anyone who owns a green pickup?" he asked. "A drab green. It's probably about ten years old, battered, and it had a dog box in the back last night."

"I've seen a green truck around, but I don't know who owns it."

"You've seen it around here?" That worried him.

"Not right near here. Just around Red Oak. Why?"

Melissa explained for Gwenn. "That's what the coon hunters who gave Hank Allerton a ride back to his truck last night were driving. Derek thinks Allerton and these men were plotting to kidnap me."

"Having them show up right where Allerton was leading us seems too convenient for coincidence."

Gwenn frowned. "But nothing happened?"

"No. Daniel Boone, here, decided we'd blaze our own trail across the Smokies. Don't be surprised if Hank Allerton says something to you about your assistant and her boyfriend taking off on their own. I don't think I made a great impression on the man, and he already thinks having Jim come here is a waste of time."

Derek remembered Jim's comment. "Maybe his father feels it's a waste of time, but Allerton's good friend Orrie Andrews seemed to think it might be worth something."

"Now that's a name I've heard," Gwenn said. "He and his brother are always getting into trouble. I think one of them spent some time in jail."

"Does this Orrie drive a green truck?"

Gwenn shrugged. "I don't know."

"Also," Derek continued, "does Jim ever have any bruises on his body when he comes here?"

"Not that I've noticed. Of course, he's only been coming here for a few weeks." She finished buttering the toast and glanced over at Derek. "Jim's the kind of kid who gives bruises."

"Which might be because he's beaten so often at home. I suggested to him that he could talk to you, and Missy told him he could come here if things got too rough at home. I hope that wasn't out of line."

"No, I'd like him to talk to me." Gwenn began setting the food on the table as Melissa poured more coffee for everyone. "And he's welcome if there's trouble at home. I didn't envision this place as a safe house, but I certainly don't know anywhere else close by where the boy could go. In small communities like Red Oak, families usually take care of their own, but as far as I can tell, there's just Jim and his pa."

"Same as it was with me. Thanks, Missy," Derek mumbled as she refilled his mug.

"The name's Melissa, not Missy," she reminded him, the words barely audible. Then she looked over at Gwenn and raised her voice. "Actually, Derek did an excellent job of talking to Jim. If he ever decides to stop being my father's hatchet man, you should hire him as a counselor."

"I'm not a hatchet man." He watched her carry the coffeepot back to the counter. She hadn't forgotten last night, and she was absolutely refusing to accept the possibility that she might be seriously in danger.

The coffee mugs all refilled, the food on the table, both women sat down. "Don't y'all dare put milk and sugar on those grits," Gwenn warned with a smile, her Southern accent coming across stronger than ever. "Not if y'all wants to eat in my house."

Derek eyed the bowl of grits. It looked like Cream of Wheat cereal, a blob of butter pooled over it.

Picking up a spoon, he tried a little. The consistency was gritty, the taste a little like corn. And that was all. Added salt didn't help, or mixing it with a bite of eggs. Forgetting the grits, Derek devoured the eggs, sausage and toast. When he finished, what he hadn't liked was obvious. Not wanting to hurt Gwenn's feelings, he spooned the grits around for a while, trying to talk himself into taking another bite, but he stopped when he realized Missy was watching him.

Her grin was knowing. Teasing. Straightening in his chair, he put down his spoon and picked up his mug. A dark glare warned her not to say anything. As usual, she ignored him.

"I don't think you've made a convert to your Southern-style grits, Gwenn. Should we let him go out and play without finishing his breakfast?"

"I saw him take three bites. That's all I ask."

Gwenn was also smiling, and he felt like a six-year-old being talked to by his mother. Only he couldn't remember his mother ever smiling when he was six—or caring if he ate his breakfast or not.

"So what do you two have planned after church?" Gwenn asked, relaxing back in her chair.

Derek looked at Missy. He knew what he wanted to do—put her on a plane back to her father. Quickly, before the desire to reach over and brush the crumbs from the corner of her mouth became too strong, and before he forgot who she was and that he'd been sent to bring her home.

Melissa watched his gaze focus on her mouth and wished she knew what was going on behind his dark brown eyes. Did his look mean he was remembering the kisses they'd shared, or did she simply have egg on her face? She ran her tongue over her lips and tasted crumbs.

It figured.

Something flickered in his gaze when her tongue traced the inner line of her mouth. Of course, it could be wishful thinking on her part. If he wanted her as she wanted him, he would have kissed her the night before. Not the hiccup-scaring, all-too-quickly-over kiss he gave her, but later, in the car, when she asked for a real, honest-to-goodness, loving kiss.

"I said, do you two have anything planned for this afternoon?" Gwenn asked again, and both Melissa and Derek jerked their eyes in her direction.

"Ah," he stammered, "I was wondering, ah, if there was anything you needed done around here? I hate eating your food and taking up space in your house without contributing something."

Melissa saw Gwenn's gaze move between the two of them. *Don't go playing Cupid,* she silently ordered. It was embarrassing enough to know she'd thrown herself at the man and been rejected. She didn't need Gwenn throwing them together, too. But the woman did have that look.

"I don't have anything for you to do," Gwenn answered Derek. "Why don't you take Melissa to Cade's Cove in the park. You've only been there once, Melissa, and Derek said he'd like to see more of the Smokies."

Melissa thought quickly. "I need to do some preparation for next week. The boys want to have something ready for the school's open house. Something really 'awesome,' according to them."

"You can work on that this evening. The sun's out and it's a beautiful day. Too beautiful to stay cooped up in the house."

"Same goes for you, Gwenn," Derek pointed out. "Why don't you come along and act as our guide."

Melissa caught his meaning. He didn't want to be alone with her. Well, she could solve that. "You two go, and I'll stay here and work."

"Which would make keeping an eye on you a little difficult," he insisted.

"I don't need you watching over me like a mother hen."

Derek merely smiled, and she knew it was no use arguing. Maybe he didn't want to be alone with her, but he was going to stick to her like glue for the next two weeks. What fun.

Gwenn kept looking at both of them, grinning. Then she pushed her chair back. "I haven't been to Cade's Cove for ages. Sounds like a fun day. We'll leave after church."

Derek did the breakfast dishes. He insisted it was only right since they'd cooked. And he was dressed in his suit and tie and waiting by the door when it was time to leave for church. "Shouldn't a good Italian like you be going to Mass or something?" asked Melissa. "Won't the Pope be upset?"

"I think I was christened in a Catholic church, but that's probably the only time I've been in one. The Hulls did make me go to church with them after Dad died and I moved in with them, but that was a long time ago, so if I make a faux pas today, you'll have to excuse me."

At the church, it was Melissa who made the faux pas, when she tried to maneuver things so Gwenn was seated between them on the pew. Somehow Derek managed to ignore the obvious and fit his broad frame into the narrow spot by Melissa's side, which placed them shoulder to shoulder. It wouldn't have been so bad if it hadn't meant that for the entire service his leg was pressed against hers, his jacket sleeve touched her bare arm and the smell of his after-shave teased her into the most irreverent thoughts. There was no question about it, she was being tortured. This was her punishment for ignoring her parents' suggestions about the proper boys for her to date, for putting up a fuss whenever they tried to match her up with one of the "right kind," and for refusing to marry Paul. She was doomed to love a man who saw her as no more than an assignment, yet delighted in tormenting her with his presence.

During the service, he kept looking around, watching anyone who gave her a second glance. Melissa was sure he suspected everyone in the congregation of plotting to kidnap her. She supposed she should be relieved that he wasn't watching the women giving him second glances. The female population of Red Oak seemed most interested in the new man in town.

Afterward, as they stood in line to shake hands with the minister and wish him a good-morning, Melissa did have to admit a lot of people were looking at her. Pointing. Whispering.

By accident or not, thanks to the article in the *Gazette,* Derek had sabotaged her anonymity.

From the beginning she'd realized that being accepted into this close-knit community was going to be difficult. Now she was truly marked as an outsider. The man was mangling her life from the inside out. And even after he left, she'd never be the same.

Back at the house they changed, had a bite to eat, then headed for the Great Smoky Mountains National Park. Derek insisted on driving, and somehow Gwenn managed to get into the back before Melissa did. "You sit up front," the older woman insisted. "You'll get a better view."

With anyone but Derek by her side, Melissa would have enjoyed the view. The mountainsides were turning into a riot of color, leaves of red intermingled with greens and golds, and the vaporous haze that always hung over the peaks was no more than a pale mist. The air was pleasantly warm, the sky a clear blue and the earth a deep red, especially where it was being torn up by construction.

Traffic through Pigeon Forge and Gatlinburg had dropped to its end-of-the-tourist-season low, but they didn't stop at either town. They didn't stop anywhere until they got out at Cade's Cove and walked around the restored old cabins and homesteads. Derek stayed closed enough to keep an eye on her, but Melissa noticed he never allowed himself to be alone with her.

It was so obvious that even Gwenn commented on it. "What's going on with you two?"

"What do you mean?" Melissa glanced Derek's way. He'd moved over to look at the John Oliver cabin with its huge stone chimney.

"He can't keep his eyes off you, and you look at him as though he were God's greatest gift to women. Yet you've barely said three words this afternoon and only get close when you have to. Did you two have a fight?"

"We've had a fight since he first arrived. Gwenn, if he can't keep his eyes off me, that's because it's his job. It's only my safety he's worried about."

"Honey, when a man looks at you the way that man has been, it's not your safety he's thinking about."

"You're seeing things." Melissa lowered her voice. "Last night, I tried to get him to kiss me, and he turned me down flat. Does that sound like a man panting after my body?"

"He wouldn't kiss you?" Gwenn's eyebrows rose, and she looked at Derek.

"He has one thing in mind, Gwenn, and that's to get me back to my father."

Gwenn just kept watching Derek.

Monday Derek stayed at the house. He wanted to see what Missy actually did. Starting at 9:00 a.m., he found out.

The prekindergarten group were children who chronologically were old enough to attend school, but who emotionally, mentally or physically weren't ready. He'd put the average attention span of any child there at five minutes, give or take four minutes—and it was mostly take. Gwenn had a challenge if by the end of the school year she expected to turn fifteen unruly individuals into a group able to follow instructions, cooperate with one another and sit still. He could see where she needed Missy's help and energy. And he was amazed by how patient Missy was with the children. She'd make a good teacher.

And a good mother.

He tried to ignore that thought.

After lunch, the two women individually tutored or had special projects planned for the children who came down from the school to the house. "We work in close cooperation with the school," Gwenn explained. "Sometimes we'll have only a few children in the afternoon, sometimes half a class if the teacher needs to work with the other half. It's a challenge, but interesting. Of course, I couldn't do it without Melissa's help."

Derek knew the last comment was meant for him. Gwenn kept dropping hints that she needed Missy around. He said nothing.

When the school day was over, he went outside with Missy to greet the "Terrible Ten," as he'd dubbed her after-school group. "Don't call them that," she insisted, watching the children start their walk toward the house.

"Isn't that Jim?" Derek watched the boy leave the group to cross the street and slip behind a parked bus. "Isn't he coming today?"

"He should be." Melissa also stared in that direction.

The bus started up and moved away, and Derek could again see the boy. Jim was standing beside a drab green truck, talking to the driver—pointing in their direction. When Jim saw them looking his way, he quickly backed up from the truck, ran across the street—almost in the path of a car—then joined the others heading toward the house.

"You get into the house, Missy," Derek ordered and started across the street, heading for the pickup.

"Derek, come back here!" Melissa yelled after him.

He didn't.

Keeping to a walk, he headed straight for the truck. He wanted a good look at the driver. Someday being able to identify the man might be important.

He'd cut the distance between them in half before the driver started the truck. The muffler rumbled. Shifting into reverse, the man backed up, then made a tight U-turn, but Derek got a halfway decent look at him. In general the man could be described as big and burly. A red baseball cap covered his head and shadowed his eyes, while a thick, dark brown beard and mustache hid the rest of his face. Derek also got a good look at the truck's license plate. That he memorized.

When he turned and started back to the house, he realized Melissa hadn't followed his orders. Instead of being safely ensconced in the house, she stood on the sidewalk, and was leaning close to Jim, looking at the boy's eye. The rest of the Terrible Ten were gathered around. "How long has this been going on?" Melissa asked Jim.

"Awhile." The boy cold barely see through his left eye, the lid almost completely swollen shut and the skin around it an ugly purple. His lips were also puffy and his cheek bruised.

Derek came up beside the boy. "Did your father do that to you?"

"No."

"Then who did?"

"None of yore business," Jim slurred, his swollen lip making talking difficult.

"Zack did it," announced Reed, his pudgy cheeks flushed almost as red as his hair. "This mornin'. Zack's makin' us give him money, but Jim didn't have none."

"Who's Zack? The guy in the truck?" Derek looked the direction the truck had taken.

Jim shook his head.

"Zack lives o'er near Blueberry hawler," said Clint, waving a hand to the west.

"He don't go to school no more," his sister, Susie, added, as though that took Zack out of Melissa and Derek's jurisdiction.

"He picks on everyone," Jerry complained. The boy fidgeted and nervously looked around, as though expecting Zack to appear at any time.

"Yeah," Reed agreed. "One time he choked me nearly to death. I couldn't eat for a week."

"Even Susie won't bite him," Tommy insisted, his encounters with Susie's teeth known to all, and Clint nodded.

"This Zack takes money from all of you?" asked Melissa.

Ten heads nodded.

"Every day?"

The heads shook in unison, and Clint explained. "Just on Mondays. He takes half our lunch money."

"Says we only need half," said Reed. "So you can see why I'm always hungry."

Melissa looked at each of them, her expression compassionate and concerned. "Why didn't you ever say something?"

"We ain't snitches," Jim growled.

"How old is this Zack?" Derek felt compassion...and anger. He knew how it felt to be picked on, bullied and beaten.

"Zack's sixteen," Clint said and gave a shake of his head, flopping his long, limp, strawberry-blond hair out of his eyes.

"What did your schoolteacher do when she saw your face?" Melissa asked Jim.

"Nut'in'. I told her I fell out of a tree while coon huntin'."

Melissa looked at Derek. "I think we should report this to the authorities."

"What they gonna do about me fallin' outta a tree?" asked Jim, his surly stance clearly stating he'd stick to that story.

"You've got to report this Zack," she insisted. "Stop him from taking money from you. That's extortion."

"I sure ain't gonna say nut'in' bad about Zack," said Jerry, moving about and checking around, the look of pure fear in his eyes.

"Me either," said Reed. And the others nodded in agreement.

"I think we'd better go inside and talk about this," suggested Derek. "I think I know a way you kids can deal with this Zack without bringing in anyone else."

"Give me another two years and I'll take him out," threatened Jim.

Melissa believed the boy. And once Zack was no longer a threat, chances were Jim would take the boy's place as the local bully. Unless, somehow, she and Gwenn could change Jim's attitude. That was their hope.

While the children ate their snack, Derek took Gwenn aside, leaving Melissa with the children. From the dining room, she could see Derek as he talked to Gwenn. He kept his voice low, his words indistinguishable. Gwenn listened, glanced toward the children, nodded, then smiled.

That Gwenn and Derek were planning something without including her irked Melissa, but she wasn't going to say anything. And by the time the children finished the peanut butter-stuffed celery sticks and their milk, Derek came over to her.

Quietly he asked, "Would you mind if I took the boys outside and showed them some self-defense moves? I'll also talk to them a bit about how to protect themselves without getting into fights."

If he'd flatly told her he was going to do it, she might have argued that she had other things planned. But how could she refuse when she knew it was exactly what the children needed? "Be my guest, but don't limit it to the boys." A wave of her hand included all the children.

Outside, the six boys and four girls sat around the picnic table and on the stone patio. Gwenn and Melissa stood back as Derek took over the role of instructor. "How many of you like giving your lunch money to Zack?" he asked.

No hands went up.

"How many of you are tired of being picked on?"

Eight hands immediately shot into the air, then two of the younger children, seeing the others had raised their hands, raised theirs.

"You know, when I was twelve, I wasn't very big, and I was always being picked on. I couldn't wait until I got bigger and could show those kids a thing or two."

"And you did, didn't ya." Young Tommy spoke out, flexing his arms like a fighter and looking at Derek's well-developed arms.

"Well, by the time I was fourteen," Derek continued, making no comment to the eight-year-old, "I was pretty big. Not as big as I am now, but big enough to push a few kids around. But you know what was really dumb, what I did was I started picking on kids smaller than me, just like the bigger kids had done to me."

"So? That's the way it is," slurred Jim.

"Not if you don't have to push people around to prove you're stronger. Let me tell you about a man I know."

Melissa found it interesting to hear Derek talk about his past, about his brush with crime, his being stopped by Sergeant Hull and the effect the man had on his life. Amazingly, the children also found it interesting. Their eyes grew wide as he told of his plot to rob the local grocer.

"Bummer," groaned Clint, when Derek described his capture.

Maybe Derek didn't realize it, but if he ever decided to stop being her father's security specialist, he had a promising future as a storyteller. He put everything into his tale of crime and punishment. A change of tone, a raised eyebrow or just the flexing of a muscle and he carried his young audience with him. They laughed out loud when he told about his first meeting with the indomitable Mrs. Hull.

By the time he got to the point of his lecture, Derek had established a rapport with the children that Melissa envied . . . and respected. For a long time after he was gone, the children would remember what he'd said. What she hated was his proving, one more time, that he was the man she wanted to spend the rest of her life with.

"Remember," he said, "if you respect yourself, you don't have to pick on others. And if you're alert and think ahead, you don't need to be a victim. But if you're cornered, or caught off guard, you can still come out a winner."

"Sure—how?" demanded Jim, his bruised face clearly identifying him as the loser this day and his question filled with skepticism.

"Melissa, would you help me demonstrate?" Derek asked, acknowledging her presence for the first time since they'd come outside.

She went to his side, unsure of what he intended to do.

"Now, Miss Davenport isn't very big, is she?"

The boys agreed with that, but some of the younger children looked doubtful. Compared to them, all adults looked big.

"You kids said this kid Zack sometimes tries to choke you. Let's say I came up behind Miss Davenport." Derek placed his hands on her shoulders and turned her away so her back was to him. "And grabbed her like this—" One darkly tanned, hairy, muscular arm went around her throat. Derek's other hand went to her shoulder, holding her in place. "Try to get away, Miss Davenport."

She tried. A twist to the side was stopped by the hand on her shoulder. A slight flex of his muscles, and he was choking her. Immediately she stopped struggling and leaned back against him in an effort to relieve the pressure on her throat.

He held her in that position, her back pressed against his body, his hips tight to her spine, and she could feel every breath he took, smell his after-shave, cologne and male essence. Her position gave her a taste of what it would be like to be held against her will. A taste of fear.

Being held by Derek also gave her a taste of something else.

It was stupid; he was merely using her for a self-defense demonstration, but she was responding to him, her heart beating faster, a warm fire heating her from the inside out. She tried to remember she meant nothing to the man, but then she felt his body respond and knew that whether he liked it or not, she was arousing him. And the deep-throated, husky chuckle he expelled close to her ear acknowledged that he knew what was happening between them.

He took a deep breath, then spoke to the children. "She's my victim now. She can't get away without being choked . . . or so it seems."

Derek paused for a moment to make certain every child was listening, then he began his instructions. "Missy, put your hands on the arm around your neck, so your fingers are next to your throat. This helps protect your airway. Now, if you're ever in this position, what you want to do is catch your attacker off guard. You must move quickly, get the person off balance and escape. To start with, do the opposite of what your attacker expects. Instead of pulling away, Miss Davenport should have thrown herself back against me and sat down on my leg."

He asked her to demonstrate, and she did. The moment she threw her weight back, he moved one foot back to balance himself.

"Do you see how I've had to change my stance to balance myself?" Derek asked. "This begins to give her an advantage."

He went on to demonstrate how she could use her weight and the weak points of his hold. Then he had the children pair up and practice the exercise. Next he showed them how to protect their throats so they couldn't be choked. Then simple ways to escape if someone grabbed an arm or wrist. For each demonstration, he used Melissa as a partner.

She tried to be objective about what was happening, to find reasons why he had to hold her so close, why he needed to brush the backs of his fingers over her cheek like a lover's caress, why his breathing sounded so shallow when he hugged her close, and why his eyes were so dark and his smile so sensuous. And she tried not to let him know his fingertip trailing over her arm sent shivers down her spine, but the goose bumps that sprang up on her skin gave her away. Just as her rapid pulse did when he put his hands on her throat.

After an hour of demonstrations and practices, she was an emotional wreck. His announcement that he'd shown them enough for one day was met by groans from the children, but she was relieved. Another minute and her legs would have turned to putty.

"Time for the open-house project," Melissa announced to the boys and hurried back into the house.

Derek came in with the boys, seating himself at the table between Jim and Clint. He said nothing, simply watched her, and she finally had to sit down, her legs no longer the stable pillars she'd once thought they were.

"Are you boys still studying about the earth at the school?" she asked from her seated position.

"It's boring," grumbled Clint. The enthusiasm he'd shown listening to Derek was gone.

"What did we have a lot of that created mountains when the earth was first forming?"

"Dirt?" asked Jerry.

"Bulldozers?" suggested Reed with a snicker.

Melissa knew they were going to make it tough on her. "How about volcanoes?"

"Oh, yeah. Them too."

"How would you boys like to build a volcano?"

That caught their attention. "Whaddaya mean?" asked Jim.

"You can each build a volcano here, after school. Then the night of the open house, we can have them erupt."

Four pairs of eyes widened. Even Derek looked interested.

Melissa grinned. "Sound okay to you?"

"Yeah," the boys said in unison.

She looked at Derek. He was smiling that enigmatic half smile she loved and hated. *What are you thinking?* she wanted to ask. *What are you trying to do to me with all this holding and touching?*

After the children left, he gave her the answer. "I want to keep going over those self-defense moves with you, Missy. I want you to practice them until they're second nature to you. If ever someone grabs you, I want you to react automatically."

"Derek, give it up. No one is going to grab me."

"You're wrong." He reached out and gently touched her cheek. "Someday some man's going to realize what a prize you are and grab you so fast that your head will spin."

But not you. He'd protect her, tease her and arouse her, but he didn't want her. Melissa turned away.

Chapter Ten

Every afternoon that week Derek worked with the children, not only teaching them ways to defend themselves, but also inserting bits of his personal philosophy. His stories entertained, and the older boys became Derek's allies, the little girls his devoted followers. Friday, sitting on and around the picnic table, they listened with rapt attention as he told them about the time he'd had to bring a girl back to her father when she'd chained herself to a tree.

"What was I to do?" he asked. "There I was, on my first special assignment for the boss, facing a very stubborn fifteen-year-old who was determined not to budge."

He looked at Melissa, and she grinned, remembering that day. It seemed a lifetime ago.

"So what did you do?" asked Reed.

Derek looked at the heavy-set boy and arched a dark eyebrow. A subtle flexing of his muscles brought all of the children's eyes to his arms, and Melissa decided it was no accident that Derek had worn the dark blue

T-shirt that emphasized every muscle in his chest and arms.

"Would you believe I tore those chains apart, tossed her over my shoulder and carried her back to her papa?"

"You did?" Susie gasped, wide-eyed with the wonder of a five-year-old.

"Tore the chains apart with bolt cutters," Melissa corrected. "Don't let this guy con you kids into thinking he's Superman."

Ten sets of eyes turned to her, and Derek grinned. "Want to tell them how you know how I got those chains off, Miss Davenport?"

She glared at him.

"How do you know?" asked Jim.

She should have kept her mouth shut. She could tell the children wouldn't be satisfied until she explained. Stepping over next to Derek, she finished the story. "I know because I was the girl. I was with a group who wanted to save some trees from being cut down. Some very old, very beautiful trees the city felt were too close to the road. So the day they were scheduled to start cutting, we each took a tree and chained ourselves to it. Then along comes this brute."

She pushed Derek's arm, and the girls giggled.

"To save the fair damsel," Derek responded with a grin.

Melissa shook her head. "Saving the fair damsel my—" she looked at the children, knowing they were waiting for her to say a swear word; she fooled them "—foot. What you were doing was jumping at my father's command."

"He did pay my salary."

"Did?" she repeated, arching an eyebrow.

"Does." And that was the problem.

"You still jump," Melissa said somberly, staring deeply into his eyes.

"I do my job."

"So how did he get the chains off you?" Clint interrupted.

Melissa's gaze shifted back to the children. "Mr. Vincetti here went to the local hardware, bought a pair of bolt cutters and cut me loose from my tree."

"Did he throw you over his shoulder and carry you back to your father?" asked Susie. Clearly she hoped that part of the story was true.

Once again Melissa looked at Derek, remembering how humiliating and exciting it had been when he picked her up. She had dreamed of being in his arms—but not like that. "He didn't exactly throw me over his shoulder, but he did carry me to his car."

"Kicking and screaming," Derek added. "Your teacher can really put up a fuss when she wants to."

"Did they cut down the trees?" asked Tommy.

"Yes," answered Melissa.

"You should have let her stay." The eight-year-old boy sounded angry.

But when he answered, Derek looked at Melissa, not Tommy. "Wanting to do something good is great, but that doesn't always mean you'll win. Sometimes the dragon wins."

And he was the dragon who planned on winning, while she was Don Quixote, battling windmills. This time the trees were children, but he saw her efforts with them as futile as fighting city hall. Just as before, he planned on taking her back to her father.

Chin high, she stared back at him. She'd proved him wrong. This time he wouldn't carry her off. One week had gone by and nothing had happened to indicate she was in any danger—other than losing her heart to a man who didn't care. One more week and he'd have to go back to her father empty-handed, and she'd stay at the Learning House, seeing what she'd started to the finish.

"Are you two gonna get married?" asked Susie.

Melissa jerked her head in the little girl's direction. "Why do you ask that?"

"'Cause you're always lookin' at him, and he's always lookin' at you."

"I'm supposed to look at her. Look *after* her." Derek emphasized the one word, grinning. "That's my job—to keep an eye on her."

"What are ya, her bodyguard?" asked Clint.

"For a while, yes."

"How come ya need a bodyguard, Miz Davenport?" questioned Reed, popping a candy into his mouth.

"'Cause she's rich," muttered Jim.

Melissa knew she had to kill that idea. "I am not rich. My father has a lot of money, but that's his money. You kids know what that's like, don't you? Just because your father has money doesn't mean you have it, does it?"

"My pa don't give me nut'in," grumbled Clint. "He don't even live with us anymore."

"Pies are ready," Gwenn called from the kitchen. "Anyone out there hungry?"

Ten children ran straight for the back door, leaving Derek and Melissa alone by the picnic table. She faced him. "If you're still trying to convince me that this job is like my other misadventures, give it up, Vincetti."

"And if you're trying to convince me you're just a poor little working girl, you can forget that, too, Davenport."

"That's all I was until you showed up... and that's all I'll be after you leave." Turning, she walked away.

Missy a poor little working girl? Derek scoffed at the idea.

He sat alone in the living room. Melissa and Gwenn were already upstairs preparing for bed. The television was off, the only sounds the water running in the pipes and soft footsteps above. Leaning back in the easy chair, he let his thoughts wander back to that afternoon.

No matter what Missy said, her situation wasn't anything like Clint's or like that of any of the other children who came to the Learning House. She'd been raised with a silver spoon in her mouth, had enjoyed every advantage a child could have, and her father would give her just about anything she wanted if she'd simply do as he asked. It was silly for her to work here.

Yet she did work.

From early morning to late at night, she put forth all of her energy devising new ways to motivate and enlighten. She made lengthy lesson plans and she improvised. She organized, she led and she stimulated imaginations.

His especially.

It wasn't easy spending twenty-four hours every day of the week under the same roof with a woman who could arouse him with just a smile. He'd thought living with Melissa would prove her pretty looks and ever-cheerful attitude to be a facade. It had worked that way with Carolyn. They didn't make it through their honeymoon before he saw her selfish, self-centered side. But with Missy there didn't seem to be a facade. She said what she thought and did what she felt was right.

Just as he had to do what he felt was right.

Derek glanced at his watch. It was after eleven o'clock. Every evening, with the exception of the night they'd gone coon hunting, after Missy and Gwenn went to bed, he called Stanley Davenport and made his report. Going to the telephone in the hallway, Derek dialed the number.

"All's fine here," he announced after the maid called Davenport to the phone. "No problems."

"There'd better not be," Davenport warned. "When are you bringing my little girl home?"

"Your little girl isn't little anymore. Your daughter is a very grown-up woman, and an excellent teacher. I've never seen anyone with more patience."

"My Missy patient?" Davenport laughed.

And Derek understood why. "I know. I never thought I'd say that about her, either. But she is. She'll go over something a hundred times if that's what it takes to teach a child. You should be proud of her."

"I am proud of her. I just want her here, where she belongs." Davenport cleared his throat meaningfully. "I'm depending on you, Derek."

"And I won't let you down." Though, for the life of him, Derek didn't know how he was going to fulfill that promise.

Saturday morning, after five days of having children around, the house seemed unusually quiet. Breakfast was leisurely enjoyed, and afterward Gwenn lingered over her coffee. As had become his habit, Derek did the dishes.

Scanning the *Gazette,* Gwenn paused and read an article, then looked up. "I assume you'll be going to the dance with us tonight."

"Dance?" He rinsed the last pan, set it in the drain and turned toward her.

"According to the *Gazette,* the dance at the town hall is Red Oak's social event of the fall. Anyone who's anybody will be there." Gwenn chuckled. "Actually, with the size of this town, I imagine everyone will be there."

"Missy's planning on going?" He certainly hoped not.

"It's Melissa, I keep telling you," Melissa said, pausing on her way through the kitchen to the back room, her arms loaded with dirty laundry. "And where am I going?"

"To the dance tonight," Gwenn answered. "I just asked Derek if he planned to go."

He kept his eyes on Melissa's face. It was safer than looking at the shapely legs exposed by her shorts. "I don't remember you mentioning a dance."

Melissa grinned. "I knew if I did, you'd have a list of reasons why I shouldn't go."

"Darned right." He was glad she understood.

"So I decided not to say anything."

"You're not going, then?" asked Gwenn.

"Oh, I'm going. I just decided not to tell him." Melissa mischievously wrinkled her nose at Derek, smiling and showing her dimples, then continued on toward the back room and washing machine.

"Missy," Derek growled.

She poked her head back into the kitchen. "I think you meant to yell, Melissa, didn't you? And if you want to go, be ready at eight. Dress is casual."

She didn't want to argue with him, but it wasn't that easy. Derek spent most of the day trying to talk her out of going, and she spent as much time trying to ignore both his arguments and his presence. Wherever she went, he went. Whatever she did, he either helped or watched. Even giving him household chores to do didn't run him off. He simply did them.

"Someday you're going to make some lucky woman a wonderful wife," Gwenn told him after he finished the windows.

Derek chuckled, and Melissa silently agreed. As a teenager she'd fallen in love with his macho image, but now she was finding the other side of his personality—his domesticated half—just as endearing.

At seven o'clock she told him she was going to take a shower and change. As she started up the stairs, she heard him grumble something about stubborn, then he asked, "What shall I wear?"

With his choices limited to the clothes he'd brought from California and the ones he'd bought in Knoxville, he ended up wearing one of his flannel shirts, a clean pair of jeans and his boots. Melissa and Gwenn each came downstairs in a cotton blouse and gathered skirt. Gwenn's colors, as usual, were subdued, primarily earth tones, while Melissa looked like a field of day lilies.

The dance was well under way when they arrived, and the town hall was nearly filled. The four members of the bluegrass band were surrounded by an array of instruments, some traditional and some homemade. They played a spritely tune, and young and old danced.

Along the far wall of the town hall was a concession stand, tables and chairs set up nearby. The room smelled of fresh-brewed coffee, popcorn and steamed hot dogs. Kids played around the edges of the dance floor, while old people sat at the tables and clapped their hands in time with the fiddles and watched the couples dance. The noise level was high, the temperature warm and the atmosphere festive.

But the moment Gwenn, Melissa and Derek stepped through the door, heads turned their way, and the room became perceptibly quieter. "We're the outsiders," Gwenn murmured. "It will take them a while to get used to us."

She led them around the edge of the large dance area toward the tables. Melissa smiled at the people staring at her. Derek didn't. Friendly was not the image he wanted to project. Let them look at Missy, admire her and see her as the nice, congenial teacher who worked at the Learning House. It was the ones who saw her as money in the bank that he wanted to impress. He wanted them to think twice, to remember him as a force to be reckoned with.

He moved possessively close, eyeing suspiciously anyone who stared too long. Most soon glanced away, turning to each other to speak in hushed tones. Only the children continued looking. The ones who came to the Learning House grinned and waved.

"Hey, Mrs. Bradley. Miz Davenport. Mr. Vinny. I didn't know y'all was comin'," said Reed. Half a hot dog disappeared into his mouth.

"Hey, Reed," Melissa called back to him. "How's the food?"

"Good," the boy mumbled, a mixture of catsup, mustard and relish dribbling down his chin.

"We do need to work on that child's manners," Gwenn said under her breath. She smiled at Reed.

They found an empty table at the far edge of the dance floor, and Derek offered to get drinks. The moment he stepped into line, he could feel the others ahead of him tense. Some kept their eyes averted; others looked away. But not the woman in front of him. Tall, willowy and attractive, she turned and looked directly into his eyes. "Hi, ah'm Sadie Fox. Susie Belle and Clint's ma. Ah've been hearin' a lot about you this past week. All ma Susie Belle talks about is the man with the big arms."

Sadie Fox looked at Derek's arms, then smiled up at him. "Clint says yore a bodyguard. That true, honey?"

Derek half smiled. "Now, do I look like a bodyguard?"

"Maybe." This time her eyes slid down over the entire length of his body, lingering at his chest and hips. Then she looked over at Melissa. "Is she really rich?"

Derek also looked at Missy. She was watching him, just the slightest hint of a pout on her mouth. She kept insisting she wasn't rich. Why should he say otherwise? "No, Miss Davenport's not rich."

"Ah didn't think she was. Why would someone rich be teaching a bunch of dumb kids in Red Oak?"

"Your children aren't dumb," Derek said. He hated labels: dumb, slow, bad. Hear them enough and kids started believing them. He had.

"Ma kids say yore teachin' them to fight like those Ninja Turtles. Is that such a good idea? Ah mean, here they are, goin' to that house after school 'cause they're bitin' and fightin' in school, and now yore teachin' them how to fight. Honey, ah don't know about you, but that don't make a lotta sense to me."

"I'm not teaching them how to fight. I'm teaching them ways to avoid a fight and how not to get hurt if they're attacked." And he hoped he was teaching them more than that. Two weeks, however, were not going to be enough time to instill a philosophy of life. It had taken Gordon Hull years with him.

"Maybe ah should let you learn me some of that Ninja stuff. Before me and my old man got a divorce, he was always attackin' me." Again she looked at Melissa. "You and Miz Davenport gonna git married?"

"No. I'm just a—" He hesitated. "A friend. Her father asked me to stop by and see how she was doing."

"Just a friend, eh?" Sadie Fox's eyebrows rose with interest.

The woman continued talking, but Derek only half-listened. He found himself scanning the room. What he was looking for, he wasn't sure. Something out of place. Something that didn't feel right.

As far as he could tell, everything was fine. It seemed a little odd to see women dancing with women, and children mingling in and running about on the dance floor. The music wasn't familiar to him, but he liked the sounds of the mandolin and banjo and found nothing ominous or threatening about a town having a good time on a Saturday night.

It wasn't until he brought three coffees back to the table that he found something to worry about.

Missy was gone.

"Where is she?" he demanded, setting the coffees down and looking around.

"Dancing," said Gwenn, nodding toward the dance floor.

Derek finally spotted her. The man dancing with Melissa looked harmless enough, but looks could be deceiving. "Who is he? What do you know about him?"

"Sit down, Derek," Gwenn ordered and pulled a chair out for him. "Stop sounding like a worried father... or lover."

He looked down at her. "Missy and I are not lovers."

"I know you're not." Gwenn patted the chair. "But maybe you should be."

He said nothing, but he sat down, his attention returning to Melissa. The guy was holding her too close. And why was she laughing? They were moving too far away from the table. Derek didn't like it.

"You can cut in, you know. It's acceptable at these dances," Gwenn informed him.

"No." He said it too quickly, too curtly. Looking at Gwenn, he softened his tone. "This is fine. I just need to keep an eye on her."

"For her protection?"

"Yes."

"Sure." She grinned.

Derek didn't argue with Gwenn, but he was glad when the next dance was a fast one and Melissa's partner escorted her back to the table. Derek glared at the man, and he wasn't surprised when the guy quickly excused himself.

"That was fun," Melissa said breathlessly, and pulled her chair closer to Melissa. The warmth of her body made her perfume stronger, headier, and Derek wrapped his hands around his cup and stared into his coffee.

"That was Bob Sager. He works in Pigeon Forge during the tourist season, and during the winter months he hauls wood for folks around here and carves animals out of pine. He invited me over to see his carvings sometime."

Derek tensed but wouldn't look at her. She touched his arm, her hand warm. "I saw you talking to Clint and Susie's mother. What did she have to say?"

"That I shouldn't be teaching her children how to fight." Derek glanced at Melissa then. Her cheeks were flushed, her eyes bright, more brown in the dim lighting than green.

"So what did you tell her?"

"That I was trying to teach them how to avoid a fight."

"Did you mention Zack?" asked Gwenn.

Derek shook his head. "The kids said they wanted to deal with Zack on their own. Before we say anything to anyone, I think we should see if they can."

The music switched to a slow song, and Melissa squeezed his arm. "Want to dance?"

She would never know how much he wanted to take her out on that dance floor, hold her close and absorb her warmth, her vitality—her femininity. Instead, he shook his head.

He knew his refusal hurt her, but he couldn't help it. Her father expected him to bring her back. To do that he couldn't get involved. At least no more involved than he already was.

"Sorry I asked," she said sharply and stood. "I think I'll mingle. I've always found the best way to become a part of a group is to get to know the people."

"Missy—" he called after her, but she walked away and didn't look back. Two tables on, she stopped and spoke to a middle-aged, slightly balding man.

Quickly the man looked toward Derek. She said something else, and the man looked back at Melissa. Grinning, he rose from his chair and walked with her to the middle of the dance floor.

"You should have danced with her," Gwenn said. "You two are crazy, you know that?"

Derek said nothing, simply watched Melissa laugh and go into the balding man's arms. Gwenn snorted and pushed her chair away from the table. "Maybe you're content to sit here all night and stare at her, but Melissa's right—if we want to be considered a part of this community, we need to get to know these people on a personal basis."

As far as Derek was concerned, there was no need for Missy to get to know anyone personally. But that didn't seem to be the attitude of the other men in the hall. Halfway through the dance, a lanky, good-looking blond cut in. Then a short redhead. And soon there was a group of men buzzing around Melissa, like bees circling a flower, each cutting in on the other, twirling her about, laughing at whatever she was saying. Looking at her as though she were made of pure honey.

She went from one partner to the next, slow dance to fast, and Derek followed every move she made, his head beginning to ache and a knot forming in his gut. Not that he was jealous. That couldn't be possible. To be jealous would mean he cared about more than her safety, and he couldn't let himself feel that way... wouldn't let himself.

"Hey, sugar, you goin' to spend the whole night just sittin' here by yoreself?"

He looked up to find Sadie Fox standing by his side. She smiled and sat down next to him. "Yore lady friend shore does have them men pantin' after her."

"Missy...Melissa's a good dancer," he said, his gaze quickly going back to the dance floor.

"You don't dance?" Sadie asked.

"Not well." Though he'd never had any complaints.

The door to the outside opened, and Jim Allerton, his father and two men entered. Derek noticed them immediately. One was the driver of the green truck. Derek was sure of that. "See the heavyset, bearded man next to Hank Allerton," he said to Sadie. "Do you know who he is?"

"Orrie Andrews? Yeah, ah know him. He's a loser, that's what he is. Did time a few years back for stealin' a car. Now ah hear he's makin' hooch."

"And the other one with him? The shorter one with the eyelid that sort of droops."

"Billy Joe. Orrie's younger brother. He ain't much better than Orrie. Lost his eye in a fight when he was a kid. Ah don't think he's done an honest day's work since the day he were born."

Derek watched the two men scan the crowd. He could tell when they saw Missy. Billy Joe smiled and said something to Orrie. Then the two continued looking around the room. When their eyes focused on him, it was Derek's turn to smile. Quickly the two men looked away.

Jim left his father and the two brothers and skirted the dancers to join Reed and Clint by the concession stand. Hank Allerton shook his head at something Orrie said and moved away from the two. Orrie and Billy Joe looked at Derek again, then at Missy. When they exchanged a conspiratorial smile, an icy chill ran down Derek's spine.

"You'll have to excuse me," he told Sadie and pushed his chair back.

Chapter Eleven

Melissa was surprised when Derek cut in. She'd been keeping an eye on him and had seen Sadie Fox sit down next to him. Melissa had been positive Derek was going to avoid her the entire dance. Now he was taking her in his arms.

Her other dance partners had held her tentatively, as though afraid she'd break or disappear. Derek embraced her possessively. Protectively. "We're going home," he said, and his first dance step led toward the door.

"Not yet." She resisted the pressure of the hand on her back and held them where they were.

"The guy with the green truck is here." Derek gave the warning low and close to her ear.

"So?"

He took a deep breath and stopped dancing, his look penetrating. "So I don't like the way he's been looking at you."

Melissa simply smiled. "You worry too much, Derek. Relax. Enjoy the dance."

"You worry too little." Someone tapped him on the shoulder. He flared at the man. "She's through dancing."

Melissa chuckled and began moving her feet, pulling him in a circle. "You're wrong. I'm not through dancing, so either dance with me or step aside and let someone else be my partner."

"I'm not stepping aside." He kept looking over her head, but he did begin to move his feet in rhythm to the slow music.

"What's the man with the green truck doing?" she asked, knowing that was who Derek was watching.

"They're watching us."

"They?"

"Orrie Andrews and his brother, Billie Joe. Look to your right when I turn you."

He made a half turn, and she looked to her right. She had to admit, the two men standing near the wall, staring their way, did give her the creeps. But she wasn't going to say that to Derek. "I think I prefer the bearded one to droopy eye."

Derek grunted his reply.

She rubbed her right hand over the back of his shoulder. His muscles were taut. "You know, you're not that bad a dancer, Mr. Vincetti, but you're really too tense. Come on, get into the swing of it. This is one of those 'Oh, woe is me' songs. Flow with it."

Missy swayed in his arms, her cotton blouse rubbing against his flannel shirt.

"Missy, this could be serious," he warned, his voice decidedly huskier.

"I'm serious." She had been from the start.

"I don't like the way they keep looking at you."

Maybe not, but she liked the ragged sound of Derek's breathing, the way his fingers tightened around hers. "What are they going to do, run out here and snatch me out of your arms and off the dance floor? I'm safe as long as we keep dancing."

A grunt acknowledged that she had a point.

Melissa rose up on her toes and wrapped her arms around his neck, her body melding with his. *Dance with me as if you care,* she wanted to plead. *Hold me tight and love me as much as I love you.*

"Missy," he groaned, and his hands went to the small of her back, holding her close.

"Yes?" She rotated her hips and knew she was arousing him. Mr. Derek Vincetti might tell her there was nothing going on between them—that she was no more to him than the boss's daughter—but his body kept telling her differently.

Pressing her cheek against his shoulder, she closed her eyes and breathed deeply. He smelled good, manly. Flannel and denim suited him as well as silk shirts and wool suits. The man would look good in nothing.

The idea of Derek in the buff made normal breathing difficult, her skin hot and her legs weak. Someday she'd have to stop torturing herself over him, but not now, not while they were finally dancing. The sound of each breath he took whispered softly in her ears. Never again would she hear a slow country-western ballad and not think of this moment. Never again would she love a man as she loved Derek.

And then the song ended and the singer cleared his throat and announced it was time the band took a break. This time Derek didn't give her a chance to resist. "We're leaving," he said with a finality that forestalled any arguments. "Let's find Gwenn and find out what she wants to do."

Gwenn wanted to stay. "But you two go on. I'll find a ride back," she insisted. The man beside her smiled, and Melissa knew Gwenn wouldn't be back until late.

"Stay by my side, Missy," Derek ordered, steering her toward the door.

"Yes, dear." She hated it when he used that overprotective tone.

Either he was too busy watching Orrie and his brother, or Derek missed the sarcasm in her answer. He said nothing until they were in the car and on their way back to the house. Checking the rearview mirror, he expelled a breath of relief. "I don't think they followed us."

"I don't think they were after us to begin with." Not that she minded leaving the dance early. Socializing for the sake of the Learning House was fine, but the only man she wanted to be with was Derek.

Back at the house, he looked up and down the street before pulling the front window's drapes closed. Melissa sat on the bottom step of the stairs, watching him. "Why are you so sure those men are after me? What have they done other than give Jim's father a lift back to his truck and show up at a dance?"

"They've been hanging around here all week."

"Not here, down by the school. If there's a problem, it may be there." Monday she would mention the truck and the two men to Mrs. Fisk, the school principal.

Derek faced her. "Missy, I know you think I'm being paranoid, but there's something about them that makes me uneasy."

He looked so sincere that she was tempted to believe him. Then she remembered who paid his salary. "Don't give me that garbage. You know I'm perfectly fine here—you're just doing this so the end of next week you'll have an excuse to drag me back to my father. Damn you, Vincetti, I thought you'd play fair."

"This isn't a game."

He stepped toward her, and she rose to her feet, standing tall and straight. "No, you're right. This isn't a game. This is the job I want, the work I've trained for. Why should I have to give it up just because my parents have other plans for my future?"

"When are you going to grow up and talk to them, face-to-face, instead of telling them lies, going behind their backs and running off half-cocked?"

His words hurt. Derek didn't understand how many times she had tried to talk to her parents, had told them her dreams. Only they wouldn't listen. "I—" she started, then stopped. With a shake of her head that tossed her hair about her shoulders like a golden-brown collar, she gave up arguing. "You know what, Derek? Talking to my parents is a lot like talking to you. I don't get anywhere. Good night. I'm going to bed."

She expected him to follow her up the stairs, but he didn't. And as exhausted as she felt, she also expected to fall right to sleep, but she couldn't. Tossing and turning, she tried to remember exactly how Orrie Andrews and his brother had looked at her. Watched her.

Was she being naive? Unfair to Derek? Was she snapping at him because he wasn't falling at her feet, wasn't in love with her as she was with him?

Finally Melissa heard Gwenn come in, the clock on the dresser showing it was after midnight. A half an hour later, Gwenn and Derek came up the stairs talking, their voices low and their good-nights to each other whispered. Melissa heard him enter his room. Lying on her bed, she could hear him moving about in the next room, could imagine him undressing. She knew when he walked over to the window and opened it a crack, and when he returned to his bed. There was the sound of springs squeaking when he lay down, then again when he rolled over. Actually over the next hour, the bed squeaked quite a bit, and Melissa knew Derek wasn't falling asleep any easier than she was.

She wasn't sure when she did finally doze off, but suddenly something woke her. With a start she sat up in bed and stared at the clock. It said two-thirty, and the house was dead still.

But something was wrong.

Not bothering to put anything on over the knee-length nightshirt she wore, Melissa padded quietly to her bedroom door, opened it a crack and listened. A faint, scratching sound came from the downstairs area. She opened her door wider, listened, then inched her way to the top of the stairs. Every step of the way she held her breath, her heart pounding in her ears and her mind racing. One wrong sound and she'd yell for Derek and Gwenn.

Looking down, she could see a light on in the kitchen, its glow illuminating the entryway and bottom stairs. Either it had been left on or turned on. One step at a time, she started down the stairs, tensed and ready to go flying back up, straight to Derek's room.

A tinkling sound, like glass falling, stopped her foot midair. She turned back toward the bedrooms.

Then from below, she heard Derek swear, and Melissa relaxed and headed straight for the kitchen.

Derek stood by the sink, his back to her, the water running. He was wearing only his jeans, and the light above picked up the ripple of his back muscles as he moved his arms. "What are you doing up at this hour?" she asked, stepping through the doorway.

"Don't move!" he warned, spinning around to face her and holding up his right hand. Instantly blood trickled down his index finger toward his palm. "I broke a glass."

Melissa stared at his hand, then at the floor. By the wastebasket was the broom and dustpan. "I don't see any glass."

"I think I got most of it."

Derek turned back to the water, and she cautiously moved across the linoleum toward him. "How badly did you cut yourself?"

"It looks worse than it is." He glanced her way when she stopped beside him. "I nicked it when I was picking up a piece of glass."

"I'll get something to put on it."

Derek's eyes darted to her bare feet. "Be careful. I might have missed some."

Melissa got bandages from the cupboard where they kept the first-aid supplies, then a towel, and while Derek dried the cut and put pressure on it, she gave the floor another sweeping. Certain they could move about without danger, she looked at the cut on his finger.

"What are you doing up at this hour?" he asked, watching her pull the covering off a bandage.

"I don't know. Something woke me." Carefully she placed the bandage over the cut, the gauze turning red as soon as it touched his skin.

"Probably me swearing when I dropped that glass."

"What are you doing up at this hour?" She tightened the bandage to put pressure on the cut.

"I couldn't sleep."

Leaning over, she kissed the tip of his finger, her hair falling over his arm and brushing against his stomach. She heard him suck in his breath, and slowly she lifted her head, smiling just slightly when her gaze met his. "There, all better."

He was still holding his breath, watching her, the look in his eyes dark and unfathomable. She reached out and touched his chest, her fingers splaying across a wall of hard muscle and catching in springy dark hairs. Beneath her fingertips the beat of his heart was strong and fast, and she knew when he did take a breath, the sound ragged.

"Derek?" She whispered his name and automatically moved closer.

His good hand went to her hair, his fingers combing into a thick tangle of locks to cradle the back of her head. Never looking away, he drew her to him. "I stayed downstairs until Gwenn came home just so I wouldn't be tempted to go to your room and do this."

His voice was husky, the confession pained. Sliding her hands to his shoulders, Melissa rose on her toes, letting her body touch his. "Think of all the time you wasted. How much time *we've* wasted."

He didn't waste any more time. His kiss was rough—possessive and demanding—and she loved it. He'd tried to avoid temptation and had failed. He'd pretended he didn't care, but he did.

Leaning back against the counter, he molded her to him, the injury to his finger forgotten as his hand moved over the back of her nightshirt, drawing it higher on her thighs. His kisses turned gentler, more probing, and she let her hands roam over his shoulders and arms, feeling his strength. For the first time in a week, he wasn't denying how he felt. He did want her, did need her.

"Oh, Missy," he groaned and paused for a breath, his eyes scanning her face. "What a mess I'm getting myself into."

"By kissing me?"

"By wanting what I cannot have."

Her heart pounding in her ears, she offered the one thing she'd denied all other men. "Derek, you can have anything you want."

"How I wish." He kept kissing her face, lightly touching his lips to her cheeks, then her forehead. Nibbling. Tasting. "Honey, in case you've forgotten, you're the boss's daughter. Forbidden fruit."

"Derek, forget my father." Maybe it would take her family a while to accept him, but in time they would.

"I can't." He stopped kissing her, but held her close, his hand moving slowly down her back to her bottom.

She reached up and touched his face, the stubble on his chin rough. Lightly she brushed her thumb over the lips that had just bruised hers. He was such a dichotomy: rough and soft. Tender and tough. Rogue yet the gentleman.

"I can't forget the differences in our backgrounds," he said solemnly. "Or that I was sent here to save you, not seduce you."

She grinned. "I don't need saving, and we're not all that different."

"Sweet Missy." He said the word so lovingly that she didn't care that he refused to give up the nickname. "I don't know what you think you see in me, but Carolyn discovered one thing during our marriage—you can polish a stone, and it may look pretty good on the outside, but inside it's still a stone."

"Maybe Carolyn didn't know how valuable a good, solid stone can be."

The way he looked at her, she knew her words had pleased him. Tucking her head against his shoulder, he blew a kiss into her hair. "You're a gem," he whispered, then sighed.

Though he held her close, she could feel him pulling away. "Derek, don't put a wall between us," she pleaded.

His voice was level when he spoke. "I promised you two weeks, and I'll give you that, but when I leave, I want you with me. Not only for your safety, but because you need to talk to your father."

"I've been thinking about that." She tilted her head so she could look up at him. "Thanksgiving isn't that far away. I'll fly home then and talk to my folks. I don't really think it will help, but you're right, I've got to give it a try."

"Thanksgiving's too far off. I didn't mean to put you in danger here, but I have. Maybe you don't feel it, but I do, and I've always trusted those feelings."

"Derek, I don't want to keep going over this." She pushed herself back, away from his warmth and strength. "I am not in any danger here."

His gaze skimmed over her green-and-yellow striped nightshirt. Slowly he grinned. Provocatively. Seductively. "You may be in more danger than you think. Get upstairs while you can."

"Or you'll what?"

He stared at her for a moment, then shook his head. "Ask me that after I've taken you back to your father."

Disappointment cut through her; nothing had changed. For a moment she silently wavered, emotions warring with commitments. Finally she spoke. "Then I guess I'll never know because you won't be taking me back."

Chapter Twelve

Sunday dawned cloudy, and by afternoon it was raining. The air was nippy, and the atmosphere gloomy—inside and out. Even Gwenn's attempts at conversation failed. Derek avoided being alone with Missy and said little. As long as she kept insisting she wasn't going back with him, what more was there to say?

She did call her parents. He overheard her side of the conversation and could imagine what Stanley Davenport was saying. Later Davenport called him, and Derek's suspicions were confirmed.

"I told her I wanted her home now, and you know what she said?" The older man's voice kept rising, and Derek held the receiver away from his ear. "She told me she'd come home for a couple of days in November. Are you bringing her back next week or not?"

"The agreement was if she was in danger she'd come back with me next week."

"So can't you make her think she's in danger?"

"I don't work that way."

"Well, if you don't bring my daughter back, maybe you won't be working at all."

Never had the man sounded so unreasonable. Davenport's attitude left Derek with a ringing in his ear and a better understanding of Missy's reluctance to face her father. It also made him seriously think about his future.

That evening he talked to Gwenn.

Melissa felt left out, yet there was no way she was going to break into the conversation Gwenn and Derek were having. Occasionally she'd looked up from the book she was pretending to read to glance toward the dining room. The two of them had been seated at the table for over an hour, talking in hushed tones. Whatever the topic, it involved her because every so often they'd glance her way. Then, seeing she was watching, they'd look away.

She went to bed early. Too little sleep the night before had left her exhausted. But she might as well have stayed up. She couldn't go to sleep until she heard Derek go to his room.

"Fool!" she chastised herself, punching her pillow. She was sure nothing was going on between Derek and Gwenn, yet she was jealous. He would talk to Gwenn; that was more than he'd now do with her.

Monday morning it was business as usual. Melissa did her exercises, showered and dressed and finished her breakfast before Derek and Gwenn came downstairs. By the time the prekindergartners arrived, the house had been transferred from a home to a place of learning. But that afternoon, when the Terrible Ten came through the door, all teaching was put on hold as each of the children clamored for Derek's attention.

"You oughta have seen him," said Jerry, jumping about.

"Jim was great," bragged Clint.

"That Zack didn't know what happened." Reed was grinning from ear to ear.

"So what did happen?" asked Derek, leading the group into the living room and settling himself down on the couch.

The children sat beside him, on the chairs and on the floor. "You tell him," Clint urged Jim.

"Well—" The boy sat taller in the easy chair. "I did like you said. I came to school like I usually did, cut across the hawler and up behind the Dickerson farm. And there he was, same place as last week, by the old shed, jist waitin' to take my money."

"But Jim didn't give him none," piped up Susie, leaning forward on the couch so Derek could see her.

"How do you know that?"

"'Cause we kinda watched," confessed Tommy, glancing at the others for approval that it was all right to tell. "We kinda hid in the shed."

"But I didn't know that," said Jim, bringing the attention back to him. "And neither did Zack."

"Not until he was flat on his back." Clint patted Jim's back. "Put there by my good buddy, here."

Jim grinned proudly. "I did just like you told me. I made him come to me, and I didn't do nut'in' until he took a swing at me. Then I just grabbed his arm, stepped away and back and pulled down. He was on the ground afore he knew what happened."

"And he was mad," said Reed. "Real mad."

"He shore was, but I kept thinkin' of what you said—" Jim looked Derek square in the eyes. "About fightin' with yore head not yore fists. Every time he come at me, I was ready."

"And when we all came out and told him we was through givin' him our money, he took off a swearin' like a hog farmer," said Clint, as pleased as though he'd been the one to whip Zack.

"You know it's not over yet. He'll try again, if not with Jim with one of you other kids. You're going to have to stick together, support each other and always think with your heads,'' Derek told them, tapping his own forehead.

''And you'll show us more Ninja stuff?'' asked Jerry, hopping up and making a few karate chops with his hands.

''Sure. While I'm still here, and as long as Mrs. Bradley and Miss Davenport don't mind.''

The children all looked over at Gwenn and Melissa. Melissa knew she didn't mind. ''Just as long as the boys get their volcanoes done for Thursday night, it's fine with me.''

''Mine's almost done,'' each boy assured her, almost in unison.

''Then there's no problem.''

She supposed she should be glad he chose Gwenn to help him demonstrate the newest self-defense tactics. Every time Derek had put his arms around her the week before, Melissa had prayed for the strength not to make a fool of herself and wished he'd use Gwenn instead. Now that he was, she felt left out.

Left out, alone and frustrated. Those were the feelings she experienced most of the next two days. Derek managed to keep as much distance between them as living in the same house allowed, and it wasn't until Wednesday night that they were alone.

The children were gone, and Gwenn had run to the store for supplies. The afternoon had been spent testing the finished volcanoes, and while Melissa sponged up the last of the red food coloring, baking soda and vinegar that made the volcanoes' lava flow, Derek carefully stored the papier-mâché mountains in the back room.

''The boys seem excited about tomorrow night,'' he said, returning to the dining room.

Melissa put the centerpiece back on the table. ''Demonstrating their volcanoes to the parents will give them a sense of importance. And you know as well as I do, those boys need all the positive strokes they can get."

"You're a good teacher."

Surprised, she turned to face him. "I never expected to hear you say that."

"They like you."

"And I like them." She moved over to where he stood. "They like you, too. You know how to hold their interest, how to explain things, get a point across without lecturing. You talk to them, not over their heads or down to them. That's a rare talent."

"Funny, I never thought I'd say this, but I'll miss them when I leave. And they're going to miss you. Have you told them?"

"Derek, I'm not leaving."

Just the hint of a smile curved his mouth, a sexy, knowing smile that curled her insides.

"I mean it," she insisted, and turned away, afraid the thought of his leaving in two days would be her undoing.

"You have to go."

He said it so sincerely that she looked back. "Derek, I can't leave. Not now, not when Gwenn needs me."

"I promised your father I'd bring you back."

"Well, you'll have to hog-tie and drag me there because I won't go willingly. Not until Thanksgiving. And don't give me the 'you're in danger' bit." She was tired of that. "I'm surprised you didn't fake a kidnapping just to get me to go with you."

That she thought he would do such a thing hurt him. "As I told your father, I don't work that way."

"So he suggested it. Figures."

Missy started for the kitchen, but Derek stopped her with a hand on her arm. "Maybe you aren't in any danger. I don't know." He hadn't seen Orrie Andrews or his brother since the dance, and he was beginning to wonder if he hadn't been overreacting. "Ever since I got here, you've had me confused."

More than she'd ever know. "I've tried not to get involved with you."

She caught a slight quaver in his voice and looked deep into his eyes. If he thought he was confused, he ought to climb into her head. "Why don't you want to get involved with me?"

"Because you're Missy Davenport... or Melissa, if you prefer."

"Meaning?"

"Meaning I work for your father."

"That shouldn't make any difference in how we feel about each other."

"Then come back with me Saturday... for our sake."

"Oh, Derek," she groaned. "Don't do this to me."

He had to. "Last Saturday night you said I could have whatever I wanted. Well, I want you to go back with me, work things out with your father. Then if you still feel anything for me, if you think there's a chance for us—"

Derek didn't finish. Let her imagine whatever she chose; he didn't think she'd come to him. Not once she was back with her family.

"You're not being fair." Melissa leaned against him, suddenly very unsure what to do. "I made a promise to Gwenn. She needs me."

Wrapping his arms around her, he held her close. Happiness was a fleeting thing. Someday he'd remember this moment, the feel of her, the smell of her hair, the way she curled her fingers into his shirt.

Someday when he was alone he would kick himself for being noble.

"I love you, Derek," she whispered.

"Tell me that after you've seen your father."

She pulled back and looked at him. "In other words, if I want you, I have to go back with you."

"Do you see any other way?"

Only one. For him to stay in Tennessee, with her. It was a pipe dream. A child's dream. Reality wasn't as easy. "I'll think about it."

Thursday afternoon excitement ran high with the Terrible Ten. The boys and Derek carried the volcanoes down to the school gym and set them up on a table, while Melissa and Gwenn helped the other children pin stories they'd written and pictures they'd drawn on the corkboard the principal provided for the Learning House students. On the wall behind the table and corkboard they taped the words LEARNING HOUSE.

Standing back, Gwenn admired the display. "I think if you stand near the table and I stand near the board, we should be visible enough so anyone with questions can talk to us."

"Do you think many of the parents of our kids will show up tonight?" Melissa looked across the gym at the children. They had gotten Derek to let down the climbing rope, and Jim was shimmying up, Derek keeping an eye on the boy.

"We'll have a lot of the mothers come just to see him," Gwenn said, chuckling. "I've noticed Susie and Clint's mother now comes into the house to pick them up. And isn't it interesting how she always has a question to ask Derek?"

"Well, now you know how to get the mothers involved. Next time don't hire someone like me, hire a hunk."

"Are you going with him Saturday?"

Melissa sighed and glanced at Gwenn. "Up until yesterday, I would have said no. Now I don't know what to do. I made you a promise I'd stay until June. You need me. But—" Could she let Derek leave without her?

Gwenn touched her arm. "I don't want to lose you, but if you want my advice, go with him. They don't make them any better than that man."

"Hey, look at me!" yelled Jim, waving at them from the top of the rope.

Derek waited until Melissa and Gwenn waved back at the boy, then he stepped nearer the rope. "Time to come down so someone else has a chance."

"Betcha no one else can make it up this far." Jim hung on for another second, then began his descent.

As soon as the boy was standing by his side, Derek gathered the others closer. Although the width of the gym separated them, he kept his voice low so Missy couldn't hear. "I don't know if Miss Davenport has said anything to you kids, but Saturday she and I are leaving Tennessee and going back to California."

"You're really leavin'?" Tommy looked stunned and tears filled his young eyes. Quickly he turned away.

"We're both leaving," Derek explained to the group. "We have to."

"For how long?" asked Reed.

"I'm not sure. Miss Davenport has to talk to her father. She may not come back."

"Is he makin' her go home?" Clint had a way of seeing to the heart of a problem.

"Sort of," answered Derek.

"I don't want you to go." Tears filled Susie's eyes and she wrapped her small arms around his leg.

He stroked the five-year-old's fine hair and spoke to all of the children. "I don't want to go, either. And neither does Miss Davenport. But we have to. Maybe we'll come back."

Clint scoffed at the idea. "That's what my pa said when he left. He ain't come back."

"Just in case Miss Davenport doesn't come back, I think it would be nice if you gave her a card or something tomorrow. What do you think?"

"Can we give you a card, too?" asked Susie.

"Sure, I'd like that. Now, give me five, and let's see who goes up this rope next."

From the other side of the gym, Melissa watched as each of the children slapped Derek's hand. "Now, what's going on?" she asked Gwenn.

The older woman looked over at the group and shook her head. "Who knows."

Melissa chose a bright red dress to wear for the open house and pulled her hair up off her neck, taming her curls into a soft twist. She wanted to stand out in a crowd, to look professional yet also approachable. The more people knew about what they were doing at the Learning House, the more chances they'd have to make the program a success.

All three of them were ready to go down to the school at ten to seven—Gwenn in a brown suit and Derek in his gray pin-stripe—when someone started pounding on the front door. Gwenn opened it, and Jim Allerton rushed in. Breathlessly he gasped, "Mr. Vinny, I gotta talk to ya."

The boy's face red and sweaty, he stumbled over to Derek. "They're gonna kidnap her." Jim pointed to Melissa and relayed his message as he sucked in air. "They're at my house now, talkin' about it. I heard 'em. They're gonna grab her at the open house and take her someplace until they get some money."

"Who is?" demanded Derek, helping the boy stand until he'd caught his breath.

"Orrie and Billy Joe. They was at our place, drinkin' with Pa, talkin' about it. I come runnin' as fast as I could. Whatcha gonna do?"

Derek and Jim looked at Melissa, and she grinned. When Jim first came through the door, she was honestly worried for the boy. The way he was breathing so hard and his flushed face, she'd really thought there was a problem. Now she knew better.

"Nice try, Vincetti," she said calmly.

Jim's expression said he didn't understand, but she knew Derek did. And she wasn't surprised by his protest. "This is for real, Missy."

"Sure. And why have the Andrews brothers decided on tonight? Why kidnap me at an open house where there'll be a lot of people around? Why not wait until this weekend, after you're gone?"

"'Cause they know yore leavin' with him after tomorrow," answered Jim.

"Oh, yeah? And how do they know that?" She didn't look at Jim but at Derek.

Nevertheless, it was Jim who answered. "'Cause he told us ya were. Just this afternoon. It were after I said somethin' to Pa about it that they started talkin' about ya."

"About ways to kidnap me, right?" She shook her head at the boy, then looked back at Derek. "You didn't trust me to choose to go with you, did you? No, you had to go and set this up."

"Missy, I had nothing to do with what Jim's saying."

"Sure." She started for the door. "Not a bad piece of acting, Jim, but Derek's little game isn't going to work. Coming, Gwenn?"

Gwenn held back. "Maybe you shouldn't go, Melissa. Those Andrews brothers are just the kind who might try to kidnap you."

"Et tu, Brute?" She was beginning to feel a bit like Caesar.

"Missy, this is not a setup. The boy's not kidding," insisted Derek. "If he says he overheard those two plotting to kidnap you, I believe him."

"They was. Honest they was," Jim repeated anxiously, looking between Derek and Melissa.

"Fine. Then let them try to kidnap me. I'm going to the open house, with you people or not."

She reached for the doorknob, but Derek moved faster, his hand clasping her wrist. Only he'd taught her well. With a twist of her arm and a quick jerk as she stepped back, she slipped out of his hold. "You are not going to stop me."

"Missy...Melissa." He had to convince her this threat was for real. "I cannot allow you to go to that open house. I was sent here to protect you."

"No, you were sent here to bring me back to my father, and you'll do anything to achieve that, won't you?"

"How can I convince you this is for real?"

"You can't," she said and again reached for the doorknob. "So if you're going to protect me, you'd better come along, because I'm leaving."

She had to fight back the tears. Walking down the sidewalk toward the school, she mumbled dozens of expletives and oaths. She'd believed in Derek. Idolized him. Loved him. But to him, she was simply an assignment. Maybe she could stimulate him sexually, but he could control a little physical attraction, use it to his advantage.

That was all his kisses had been. A way of throwing her off balance, of confusing her. Well, she was completely confused now—and hurt—but she'd go through this open house with a smile, and then she'd send her daddy's flunky home, as she should have two weeks ago.

In the gym, Derek stayed as close to her as he could without standing in her shoes. Her anger was visible, from her ramrod stiff posture to the dark green of her eyes. Standing by the table of volcanoes, she said nothing to him, but he knew she was thinking every vile thought possible.

She was the one about to erupt, and he was caught between a rock and a hard place. No matter what happened tonight, she'd think he set it up...or called it off. Which left him with only one alternative—to protect her.

Continually scanning the crowd in the gym, he watched for Hank Allerton, Orrie Andrews or his brother Billy Joe. He was keeping an eye on the door to the hallway when Susie and Clint's mother came over and tapped him on the arm.

"The kids tell me you and Miz Davenport are a-leavin'." Sadie Fox glanced at Melissa, then smiled up at him. "Ahm truly gonna miss y'all. Our little talks have helped me understand ma Susie Belle and Clint. Ahm tellin' ya, it's not easy raisin' two kids without a man around."

The woman dropped her voice to a sultry pitch and inched closer. "Ah was thinkin', honey, maybe afore you leave Red Oak, you and me could go out for a little drink or somethin'. Like a thank-you for yore help."

"I don't think so," he answered quickly, all the while trying to think of an excuse. "I...Miss Dav—"

Melissa moved away from the table, and he stopped midsentence. She was heading for the hallway door. "Where are you going?" he called after her.

She ignored him and kept walking.

"Melissa!" he bellowed.

Not only did she stop, but half the people in the gym turned toward him and her. Leaving Sadie's side, Derek strode to Melissa. "Where are you going?" he repeated, this time the words low and strained.

She tossed her head and lifted her chin defiantly. "To the little girls' room, if that's all right with you, Mr. Vincetti. And please don't tell me you plan on following me in there."

"No, but I'll wait for you outside."

She snorted in disgust and started walking again. He followed, positioning himself by the door to the bathroom. He didn't like having her out of his sight, but he wasn't about to make a total fool of himself and go in with her, not with a group of giggling school-aged girls already in there.

He was waiting for Melissa to come out when the school principal came rushing down the long hallway. Never one to raise her voice, Mrs. Fisk waited until she was nearly to him before calling out, "There's a long distance call for you, Mr. Vincetti. From California. The man said it was an emergency."

"An older man?" Derek questioned, glancing away from the bathroom door to look at Mrs. Fisk.

"Ah don't rightly know." Her brow wrinkled some. "Ah couldn't hear the man that well."

He didn't know what to do. Wait until Melissa came out or answer the call? He'd told Davenport they'd be at the school tonight. If Stan called here, it had to be an emergency. Pushing the door to the bathroom open an inch, he yelled in. "Melissa, I've got to take a telephone call...from your father. Stay where you are until I get back."

He hoped she heard over the squeals and giggles of the girls standing by the sinks. And he hoped, for once in her life, Melissa followed his orders.

The office was at the opposite end of the hallway. He didn't wait for Mrs. Fisk to show him the way, but covered the distance in half the time it took her. Picking up the receiver lying on the desk, he spoke before listening.

He could have saved his breath.

A dial tone was all he heard, and he knew then that he'd been tricked.

Immediately he remembered the telephone by the library, the one students used to call home. He'd had his back to it while waiting for Melissa to come out of the bathroom. A person could have easily used it to call the office. Used it and hung up and left as soon as he saw Mrs. Fisk start out of her office.

Derek slammed down the receiver and dashed past the woman as she entered the room. "Got to get to Missy!" he yelled in explanation and broke into a run.

Before he even got to the girls' bathroom, he knew Melissa hadn't followed his orders and stayed inside. Through the glass doors at the end of the hallway, he could see the school's parking lot. Outside Orrie Andrews had Melissa by the arm and was dragging her toward the drab green truck that was parked a few yards away. Billy Joe was close by and so were Jim, Clint, Reed and Jerry. The boys were after the two men and Melissa, and when Derek came barging out of the school building, he could hear their shouts and yells.

It was obvious Orrie didn't consider the boys a threat, not until Jim rammed a shoulder into his side and Clint grabbed the arm holding Melissa. Then the man yelled at his brother for help, but Billy Joe was protecting himself from Jerry and Reed, who kept coming toward him, screaming and making karate jabs in the air.

None of the boys would have been effective alone, but together they created a terrifying sight and sound, and the moment Orrie saw Derek, he stopped trying to hold on to Melissa.

She fell to the pavement, and Orrie easily shook off the two boys. Without hesitation, he dashed for his truck, Billy Joe right beside him.

Derek ran by Melissa and the boys; Orrie and Billy Joe were his target. This time there'd be no question about motives. Finally Melissa would realize his suspicions had been right from the start.

Distance, however, was on the brothers' side. Orrie was behind the wheel, starting the engine, and Billy Joe was pulling his door shut before Derek reached the truck. A sneer twisted Orrie's face as he threw the gears into reverse, and to his frustration, Derek's hand touched the smooth metal of the front fender, not the handle of the door.

The green truck bounced over the curb and onto the street, whined as it was thrown into first gear, then roared down the road. Derek took two steps after it before stopping. There was no way he could outrun a truck.

Turning, he was relieved to see Melissa on her feet again. Her red dress was smudged with dirt and her hair was in total disarray, but she looked unharmed. Jim, Clint, Reed and Jerry were proudly slapping one another on the back and shaking one anothers' hands.

Derek hurried back to them.

"We stopped 'em, didn't we?" Jim said, looking at Derek for approval.

"You guys were great," he acknowledged.

Clint stood taller than ever, grinning proudly and flexing his muscles. "They didn't know what hit 'em."

"Aagh, aagh." Jerry made two quick karate chops to the air. "Just call us the Ninja Turtles."

The one who wasn't saying anything was Melissa. Derek looked at her. "You okay?"

Her mouth a tight line, she glared at him. "Oh, just fine, no thanks to your little charade. You know, I've always thought my father was the master manipulator, but you've got him beat, Vincetti. You set this up from the very beginning, didn't you?"

Ice ran in his veins. He could follow her thinking, but pretended he didn't. "I don't know what you mean."

"Don't you? How long did it take you to plan all this? Did you already have it set up when you gave that story to Mary Sue? When you taught the kids self-defense? And just how much did you have to pay Jim's dad and the Andrews brothers to stage this little kidnapping attempt?" She looked at Jim. "How much did he pay you?"

Jim shot a look at Derek. "He didn't pay me nut'in'."

"Then you got took, kid," she said. "Just like me."

Chapter Thirteen

"You're home, at last." Helen Davenport rose from the mauve settee in the parlor, tears springing to her pale brown eyes. "We were so worried about you."

Melissa hugged her mother, and the anger that had consumed her since Thursday night was pushed aside. "I didn't mean to make you worry. That's why I called every week."

"Well, the wayward chick has come home." Her father strode into the ornately furnished room. "How could you do such a stupid, foolish thing?"

Melissa tensed and pulled back from her mother. What she'd done was foolish and stupid, all right. She'd been stupid to think she could follow a career she wanted; foolish to trust Derek, love him. In control, she faced her father. "I'm sorry. As soon as I decided to take that job in Tennessee, I should have told you and Mother the truth."

"No, you never should have accepted the job." Her father's eyes had turned a steely blue, his tone harsh.

"Of all the dumb messes you've gotten yourself into, this beats them all."

"It wasn't a mess until you sent Derek. I was doing just fine. Discovering what I wanted to know."

"Which was what?" demanded her father.

"That I like that kind of work. That I don't simply want to be a teacher, I want to intervene, make a difference."

"Honey," her mother interrupted, "if you want to help the less fortunate, you can always join our committee on illiteracy. I've even been working with a young man who can't read. But I'm doing it in a safe environment."

Safe and distant, Melissa would bet. "I want a closer involvement. What Gwenn is doing is exciting. In just a few weeks we could see a change in the children." Of course, with the ten after school, much of that change had been due to Derek's influence, but Melissa didn't want to think about that. "I went to Tennessee to see if working with the disadvantaged was what I wanted to do, and it is."

"What about Paul? The company?" her father probed.

"What about them?" She knew what he wanted. And maybe a century ago he could have forced her into a marriage of convenience, but not today. "Paul's a nice man, but I don't love him."

No, she loved a man who'd betrayed her.

If the hurt inside her showed, Stanley Davenport didn't seem to notice. "Paul's father and I have been talking about merging the companies."

"Then merge them." She didn't care.

"You don't understand," Helen Davenport said calmly. "Someday you'll inherit the business. And since you don't seem to have much of a business sense, you really need to marry a man who can take over."

Someone like Paul . . . or Derek. Melissa wished she wouldn't keep thinking of him. For a day and a half she hadn't spoken to him, wouldn't look at him except when she had to. Now that he'd delivered her safe and sound to her father, she couldn't keep his name from popping into her head.

"Daddy, I don't know what you're going to do with the business, but I'm not marrying a man just so there'll be someone to fill your shoes."

"You're not thinking logically," he snapped.

Melissa knew that for once in her life she was thinking logically. "I'm sorry. I know the company's important to you, and I can understand your concern for its future, but pairing me up with a business executive is not going to work. Maybe what you need to do is turn Davenport into a public corporation, find a good CEO to take over." She could suggest a name. Derek Vincetti. He certainly knew how to get his way. "Now, if you'll excuse me, it's been a long trip, and I'm still functioning on Eastern time. I'm going to my room."

She left her parents and went up to the room that had been hers since she was two years old. The decor and furnishings had changed over the years, but the view from her window was basically the same. Staring out, she watched Raoul, the maintenance man, skim leaves from the swimming pool. Beyond the pool was the immaculately groomed green her father used to practice his putting, then the tennis courts framed by a backdrop of the Santa Cruz Mountains.

The house was really too big for a family of three. Stanley and Helen Davenport should have had more children. Then maybe her father would have had one to share his interests and take over the business. Instead, Stanley and Helen had ended up with one daughter who felt like a misfit in her own home.

There was a knock at the door, and Melissa turned away from the window. "Come in."

"Would you like me to unpack your bags?" asked a young woman Melissa had never seen before.

"No, thank you," she said and dismissed the maid.

Servants came and went faster than she could keep track of them. Her favorite would always be the soft and round ever-smiling Maria, who had spent hours with a little girl she called Missy while Helen Davenport had her hair fixed, played bridge and lunched with her friends. But after the kidnapping, Maria had been fired. Her father had blamed the woman for not watching his daughter close enough. And no amount of begging on Melissa's part had changed her father's mind. Stanley Davenport wouldn't listen to a six-year-old.

He wouldn't listen to a twenty-three-year-old, either.

For the next week Melissa tried to make her parents understand that she was not staying. She also tried to forget Derek and what he'd done. But memories of his telling stories to the children, working with the boys—kissing her—taunted her day and night. She loved him and she hated him, and the conflict was emotionally draining. During the day she went nowhere, did nothing but sit and stare. In the evenings, she dined with her parents, sat with them as they watched television, then went to bed early.

The following Saturday, she called Gwenn. "I've had it. I can't spend another week here. I'm coming back."

"I think it's safe."

"Come on, Gwenn. We both know it was always safe, that Derek set up that little kidnapping attempt just so I'd have to come back with him."

"Melissa, he didn't set that up," Gwenn insisted. "Those Andrews brothers really did try to kidnap you. And you're lucky they didn't succeed. Today I read in *The Knoxville News-Sentinel* that they've been arrested for an assault and robbery over in Pigeon Forge."

"I..." Melissa hesitated, unsure what to believe. "No, it was too convenient. Those brothers grabbing me was just what Derek needed to make me stick to my promise to go back with him. He had to have set it up."

"Maybe it was convenient, honey, but do you really think Derek would hire those two to grab you? I can't see it. Plus, Jim's father stopped by last week. He kept telling me he had nothing to do with what happened. If ever I've heard a man protest too much, it was Allerton. He may not have been at the school that Thursday night, but I think he was in on what happened. In fact, I think Derek was right about something fishy going on when you went on that coon hunt. Instead of being mad at that man, I think you should be thanking him."

I should be loving him, Melissa realized.

The cloud of depression that had been hanging over her suddenly lifted. She did need to apologize to Derek. Ask him to forgive her.

Before the open house, he'd said she should come to him after she talked to her father. Well, she'd talked to her father—it was time to talk to Derek. "Gwenn, I'm not sure what I'm going to do, after all. I'll call you as soon as I know."

Her father had Derek's address and telephone number in his personal address book in the den. Melissa copied it down, then told her mother she had to go out. With butterflies in her stomach and her heart beating double time, she drove to San Jose.

It didn't take her long to find the apartment building, or Derek's apartment. Only no one was home. The place was empty.

"He moved out," a neighbor said. "Just last Wednesday. Said he needed to find himself." The gaunt, sallow-faced man laughed. "I didn't know he was lost."

Melissa had to wait until her father came home from playing golf before she could ask him what was up. But when Stanley Davenport walked through the door, he wasn't alone. "Missy, look who I ran into at the club. Paul. He didn't have anything planned for tonight, so I invited him over to dinner."

Melissa gave Paul about ten seconds, long enough for a, "Hello, how are you?" then she grabbed her father's arm. "Where's Derek gone?"

"Vincetti?" Her father's eyes widened a bit. "Why, he quit. I thought you knew. Surprised the hell out of me."

"When? Why?" Twenty-four hours ago, she would have sworn she didn't care. Now she had to know.

"Last Monday morning. I'd no sooner stepped into my office than he came in, handed me a letter and said he was resigning, effective immediately, that I owed him a vacation and he was taking it." Stanley Davenport looked at Paul. "We're talking about my security man. Would you believe it? The guy quit because I said I'd fire him if he didn't bring Missy home. I'm giving him a week to cool off, then I'll call him and get him to come back."

"He won't be back." Melissa knew that as surely as Derek had known she was in danger. "And you can't call him. He's moved."

"So I'll have someone find him."

"Who?" She laughed at the irony of it. The one who could best find Derek was Derek.

"We'll talk about this later," her father grumbled, then pushed her toward Paul. "Fix our guest a drink. I'm going to take a shower."

She knew it wasn't just by chance that Paul was at the house. Her father hadn't given up on his plan to marry her off to Paul and merge the companies. Once again her protests had fallen on deaf ears.

Melissa did fix Paul a drink, then she excused herself and went up to her room. Twenty minutes later, after a half-dozen telephone calls and a hasty note to her folks, given to the maid with instructions to deliver it in ten minutes, she was once again in her car on her way to San Jose.

Debbie and Gordon Hull lived on the opposite side of town from Derek's apartment. The sergeant was now a captain, and the couple welcomed her into their spacious home and invited her into their living room. There Debbie Hull brought in coffee and cookies, along with glasses of milk for the two preschoolers playing a video game.

"These are my grandchildren," she explained. "They're spending the weekend with Grandma and Grandpa. Now, what is it you wanted to ask us about Derek?"

"If you know where he is." Melissa didn't know who else to ask. "I went to his apartment this afternoon, but was told he'd moved out. And my father said Derek quit his job Monday. I've got to talk to him."

Gordon Hull leaned back in his chair and grinned. "From what Derek told us, you never wanted to talk to him again."

"You've seen him then? Talked to him?" It was her first shred of hope.

"We saw him Wednesday," Debbie Hull said. "Before he left."

"What did he say? Where is he?"

"We don't know." The captain took a sip of his coffee. "When Derek stopped by, he said he'd quit his job, moved out of his apartment and wasn't sure what he'd be doing or where he'd end up, but that he'd call us once he got settled. What happened, anyway?"

Melissa told them, starting with the day Derek showed up at the Learning House, then backtracking to when he first started working for her father. "I idolized him from the moment I saw him," she confessed, "but I don't really think I got to know the man until he came to Tennessee. Listening to him talk to those kids, watching him work with them—"

She looked at Gordon Hull. "Your friendship has meant a lot to him, what you did for him when he was younger. He told the kids about you while he was working with them, passed on some of your philosophy. Really, you should have seen him. He was great."

"But you didn't trust him, did you?" Debbie Hull spoke softly, but her words made a direct hit.

Looking down at the cup she held in her hands, Melissa blinked back tears. "No, I didn't."

"You knew his ex-wife?" Gordon Hull asked.

"Yes, I did. Not well, but I knew her. And Derek talked about her."

"She hurt him. A lot. We wouldn't want to see Derek hurt again."

Melissa looked at the two. "I don't want to hurt him. I love him." And if she could go back in time, she would. Only she couldn't.

"I wish we could help you," said Debbie Hull.

"You can," insisted Melissa. "When Derek contacts you, could you relay a message? Could you tell him I said I'm sorry, for everything. Tell him I've gone back to Tennessee, that he fulfilled his obligation. Now I've got to fulfill mine, but that I did mean it when I told him I loved him. Also, remind him that he told me to come see him after I talked to my father. I can't if I don't know where he is."

"We'll tell him," Gordon Hull answered.

Melissa's father was waiting up when she got home, and she didn't have to ask if he was angry. His eyes were a cold blue, his voice harsh and his face red. "Where the hell have you been?"

"I left you a note. Didn't the maid give it to you?"

He snorted. "I invite someone home to dinner, and you leave a note. What has gotten into you, Missy?"

"I wanted to find out where Derek's gone. I thought some people in San Jose might know."

"And did they?"

"No."

"Why do you care where Derek Vincetti's gone?"

She gave him the truth. "Because I love the man, and if I'm going to marry him, I need to know where he is."

"Marry Vincetti?" Davenport's laugh was curt. "Is that what he did while he was back there? Seduce you? Fill your head with foolish ideas? Well, let me tell you, kiddo, it's just your money he's after. And you can tell him, if he marries you, I'll disinherit you."

"So disinherit me."

"And then what will you do?"

"Work for a living, as I have since July. I'm going back to Tennessee, Daddy. I'm going to fulfill my contract with Gwenn Bradley."

"And you think Vincetti will come for you there?"

"I don't know, but I sure hope so."

"Go to bed. We'll talk about this in the morning."

They didn't talk, her father did, and then her mother. The lecture was the same. As the only child, she couldn't just ignore Davenport Computers. It was ridiculous to teach so far away. What if Derek did come after her? A man who would quit his job over a small misunderstanding wasn't the kind of man she should want. Someday she'd regret turning her back on what she could have had. She was thinking with her heart, not her head. She was being foolish.

Melissa let them talk, then she calmly repeated what she'd already told them. "I'm going back to Tennessee. I signed a contract with Gwenn to work with her until June. After June, I'll decide what I want to do. Maybe I'll come back to California and find a job somewhere around here." Especially if Derek was anywhere in the area. "Maybe I'll stay in Tennessee.

Meanwhile, Daddy, if you and Paul's dad want to merge your companies, why don't you do it? Just don't expect me to marry Paul so you can."

"But, baby, if you're in Tennessee, I'll worry about you," her mother insisted. "What if those men try to kidnap you again?"

"From what Gwenn has told me, they'll be in jail a long, long time. My chances of being kidnapped are a lot greater here than there, and I'll call every week, as I have been doing. I could even fly back for Christmas." It would give her a chance to look for Derek.

Her parents were still trying to talk her out of the idea when Melissa packed her last box of clothes into her little red compact. This time she was leaving openly, taking her car and personal belongings as she should have done the first time. Her father grumbled when she kissed him goodbye, and her mother cried, and they insisted she call every night she was on the road so they'd know she was safe. And they waved as she drove away.

Speeding cross country, Melissa knew she'd done the right thing. For the first time she'd been honest with her parents and told them exactly what she was doing and why. She was setting off on her own.

And this time she wanted Derek to come after her.

Chapter Fourteen

Melissa made great time until Goodland, Kansas. Which wasn't the good land for her. There a sick water pump cost her a tow bill and an extra night in a motel, and when she got the mechanic's bill, she was certain she'd just paid his rent for the next month and a half. It was Thursday before she drove into Red Oak.

The afternoon sun was low over the Smokies, and the air had a definite nip. Leaves of red and gold lay on the ground, the trees baring more of their branches. Jerry and Reed were in front of the Learning House, raking the leaves into piles when Melissa pulled into the driveway.

"Hey, Miz Davenport," Reed called. "Mrs. Bradley said you was comin' back."

"Had to. Had to see how you're doing with your reading."

"I'm doin' good," he said proudly. "I've been put in another book."

"Good for you."

She left her luggage and boxes in the car. Later there'd be time to unpack. Now she wanted to see Gwenn and the rest of the children.

Gwenn looked surprised when she opened the front door, then she laughed and extended her arms for a hug. "I didn't expect you until tomorrow at the earliest. In fact, from what I've heard about your house and lifestyle, I can't imagine why you've come back at all. You've got to be crazy."

"My folks think I am." Melissa waved at the children in the living room, and they came running over to greet her. When each had had a hug, she stood and looked around. Everything seemed the same—except Derek was no longer around.

Gwenn watched her and grinned. "I think you should go out back and say hi to the boys. They're raking leaves."

"In a minute." Derek had spent so much time out back, working with the children. She wasn't ready to face the memories.

"No, now," insisted Gwenn.

"Now?" The demand surprised Melissa. It wasn't like Gwenn to issue orders.

"Yes."

Obediently Melissa went to the back door, Gwenn following. She saw Jim the minute she stepped outside. Then Clint.

Then Derek.

"He arrived Monday," Gwenn said quietly. "I think you two have some talking to do. Come on, boys!" she yelled to the two. "I want you inside for a minute."

"Hey, Miz Davenport," Jim called and grinned at Derek. "Look who's here."

"I see," he said but didn't move.

"You back?" asked Clint, dropping his rake and heading for the house.

"I'm back." She couldn't tear her eyes from Derek.

He stood where he was, rake in hand. He wore a red-and-black plaid flannel shirt, the sleeves rolled to his elbows, stained jeans and scuffed boots, and he looked wonderful. His dark eyes darted from her hair to her gold blouse to her brown slacks and loafers. She imagined she looked a mess after being in a car most of the day.

"Hi," she managed after the boys and Gwenn went inside.

"Hi," he answered, leaning the rake against the side of the house.

"Did the Hulls give you my message?"

He shook his head and started toward her. "What message?"

Her heart was racing faster than her car engine ever had, and it felt like a butterfly convention in her stomach. "I told them to tell you I'd be here." *That I love you.*

"I haven't talked to them since I left California." He stopped directly in front of her. "What did you tell your folks this time? That you had another sick friend?"

"No, I said I had a contract to fulfill."

Derek loomed over her, piercing her with his gaze. Boldly she tilted her chin up and looked him straight in the eye. "I also told them I was going to marry you."

"Oh, I bet that went over great." He didn't smile.

"Actually Daddy said he'd disinherit me." She needed to know if that would matter to Derek.

"And what did you say?"

"That I didn't care."

She wished he would touch her, hold her. Kiss her. Instead he just looked at her, his mouth a tight line and his body rigid. It seemed an eternity before he spoke. "Missy, do you have any idea what being married to me would be like? I quit my job. I don't work for your father anymore."

"I know."

"I'm going back to school. Here, in Tennessee. At Knoxville. I'm going to get a master's degree in Education. Do what Gwenn's doing."

"I'm glad."

He glanced at her mouth, then went on listing the negatives. "I've made some investments over the years, but compared to what you're used to, we're talking peanuts. And teaching, I won't be earning as much as I did working for your father."

"But you'll be good. You have a lot to offer children." She wished he'd get to the point. Did he love her? Did he want to marry her?

"I'll probably never be able to afford a big house like you're used to... fancy cars... designer clothes." He let his gaze trail down over her clothing.

Melissa touched his arm. "Derek, none of those things has ever been important to me."

"No, I guess they haven't." It had taken him a long time to realize that, to stop comparing her to Carolyn. Actually he hadn't completely trusted his feelings, not until two minutes ago when he looked up and saw her step out of the house. "I'd hoped you'd come back," he confessed.

"Is that why you're here?"

"No—" Or maybe it was, he wasn't sure. "I came back to help Gwenn. She can't do all this by herself."

"I know. That's why I came back." Melissa let go of his arm. She'd opened the possibility of marriage. He hadn't given her an answer. "About what happened at the open house. I'm sorry for all the things I said that night." And for the next two days. "I guess I was wrong. It just seemed so... well..."

Nervously she fluttered her hands in the air. He caught one, entwining her fingers with his. "I guess from your point of view it must have seemed like a setup. Though you should have trusted me not to do that."

"If you'd been in my place, would you have trusted me?"

There were a lot of things he hadn't trusted her about. Her sincerity about what she was doing. Her love.

"Derek," she whispered, her heart pounding in her ears, the warmth of his hand infusing all of her body. "Am I making a fool of myself?"

"No." He couldn't draw his eyes from hers, not even as he brought her hand to his mouth and kissed her fingers. "If there's a fool, it's been me."

For the first time he smiled. Really smiled. And he drew her close. "Missy, when we were here before, I worked for your father. There were certain things in all good conscience I couldn't do or say. And some things I was afraid to believe."

"And now?" she held her breath.

"Now—"

His kiss said it all. She was back on that roller coaster, feeling the exhilaration and excitement. But this time he was with her, holding her tight, keeping her safe. A fifteen-year-old's daydreams had come true. It had just taken a while. Taken an eternity.

"I love you, Melissa," he whispered near her ear. "I want to spend the rest of my life with you. I want you to be my wife, have my children, be my friend and lover."

As his lips once again touched hers, Melissa knew they'd be lovers very soon and friends for a lifetime. And she hoped their children would all have his beautiful brown eyes and his integrity and his loyalty.

In California Stanley Davenport telephoned his wife. Leaning back in his chair, he put his feet up on his desk. "Think she's there yet?"

"She should be," Helen Davenport answered. "You're sure he's there?"

"He asked payroll to send his last check to the Learning House, Red Oak, Tennessee." Stanley chuckled. "I don't know if we're doing him any favors. He's going to have his hands full with her."

"You've always liked him, and she loves him."

"Paul would have been better for the business."

"Stanley, we've been over this."

"I know. Bringing Paul home was my last try."

"She'll be safe with Derek."

"They're both stubborn as all get-out, but I think we can come up with a little wedding present that will make their lives easier." Stanley Davenport leaned back in his chair and looked around his office. "Maybe one of our grandchildren will be interested in computers."

* * * * *

"GET AWAY FROM IT ALL" SWEEPSTAKES

HERE'S HOW THE SWEEPSTAKES WORKS

NO PURCHASE NECESSARY

To enter each drawing, complete the appropriate Official Entry Form or a 3" by 5" index card by hand-printing your name, address and phone number and the trip destination that the entry is being submitted for (i.e., Caneel Bay, Canyon Ranch or London and the English Countryside) and mailing it to: Get Away From It All Sweepstakes, P.O. Box 1397, Buffalo, New York 14269-1397.

No responsibility is assumed for lost, late or misdirected mail. Entries must be sent separately with first class postage affixed, and be received by: 4/15/92 for the Caneel Bay Vacation Drawing, 5/15/92 for the Canyon Ranch Vacation Drawing and 6/15/92 for the London and the English Countryside Vacation Drawing. Sweepstakes is open to residents of the U.S. (except Puerto Rico) and Canada, 21 years of age or older as of 5/31/92.

For complete rules send a self-addressed, stamped (WA residents need not affix return postage) envelope to: Get Away From It All Sweepstakes, P.O. Box 4892, Blair, NE 68009.

"GET AWAY FROM IT ALL" SWEEPSTAKES

HERE'S HOW THE SWEEPSTAKES WORKS

NO PURCHASE NECESSARY

To enter each drawing, complete the appropriate Official Entry Form or a 3" by 5" index card by hand-printing your name, address and phone number and the trip destination that the entry is being submitted for (i.e., Caneel Bay, Canyon Ranch or London and the English Countryside) and mailing it to: Get Away From It All Sweepstakes, P.O. Box 1397, Buffalo, New York 14269-1397.

No responsibility is assumed for lost, late or misdirected mail. Entries must be sent separately with first class postage affixed, and be received by: 4/15/92 for the Caneel Bay Vacation Drawing, 5/15/92 for the Canyon Ranch Vacation Drawing and 6/15/92 for the London and the English Countryside Vacation Drawing. Sweepstakes is open to residents of the U.S. (except Puerto Rico) and Canada, 21 years of age or older as of 5/31/92.

For complete rules send a self-addressed, stamped (WA residents need not affix return postage) envelope to: Get Away From It All Sweepstakes, P.O. Box 4892, Blair, NE 68009.

© 1992 HARLEQUIN ENTERPRISES LTD. SWP-RLS

"GET AWAY FROM IT ALL"

Brand-new Subscribers-Only Sweepstakes

OFFICIAL ENTRY FORM

This entry must be received by: May 15, 1992
This month's winner will be notified by: May 31, 1992
Trip must be taken between: June 30, 1992—June 30, 1993

YES, I want to win the Canyon Ranch vacation for two. I understand the prize includes round-trip airfare and the two additional prizes revealed in the BONUS PRIZES insert.

Name ______________________________

Address ______________________________

City ______________________________

State/Prov. ______________ Zip/Postal Code ______________

Daytime phone number ______________________________
(Area Code)

Return entries with invoice in envelope provided. Each book in this shipment has two entry coupons — and the more coupons you enter, the better your chances of winning!

 2M-CPN

"GET AWAY FROM IT ALL"

Brand-new Subscribers-Only Sweepstakes

OFFICIAL ENTRY FORM

This entry must be received by: May 15, 1992
This month's winner will be notified by: May 31, 1992
Trip must be taken between: June 30, 1992—June 30, 1993

YES, I want to win the Canyon Ranch vacation for two. I understand the prize includes round-trip airfare and the two additional prizes revealed in the BONUS PRIZES insert.

Name ______________________________

Address ______________________________

City ______________________________

State/Prov. ______________ Zip/Postal Code ______________

Daytime phone number ______________________________
(Area Code)

Return entries with invoice in envelope provided. Each book in this shipment has two entry coupons — and the more coupons you enter, the better your chances of winning!

© 1992 HARLEQUIN ENTERPRISES LTD. 2M-CPN